Seventeen
Dry
Seasons

Seventeen Dry Seasons

Tamu Mazama

Universal Write Publications LLC

SEVENTEEN DRY SEASONS

Book Designer: Author Support
Book Editor: Dr. Alice Nicholas| Temple University

For information: Website at www.UWPBooks.com

Publisher:

Universal Write Publications LLC
Mailing/Submissions Universal Write Publications LLC
421 8th Avenue, Suite 86 New York, NY 10116

This title is part of the CHEYANNE BOOK SERIES (CBS)

ISBN-13: 978-0-9825327-9-9
ISBN-10: 0-9825327-9-2

For Brother Ibo, who taught me that,
"When there is no beauty, you've got to create some."

Acknowledgments

I WANT TO THANK my beloved mother for believing in me each step of the way and for holding me when I felt like falling. You are my rock, my foundation, and thank you for giving me roots to keep me grounded and wings to give me freedom. You instilled in me a sense of purpose and mission. I am so grateful for Kiamuya, my brother, for being a great critic and encouraging me from sun rise to sun down. Also, Sister Ife for giving me the strength I needed to complete this book. I am appreciative of Sister Ama who always wants the best for me and gave me much inspiration; of Yoa and Ophelie who sent me endless love and always believed in me; and of Brother Makodou for his feedback and continuous support. I am so thankful toward Auntie Nah for teaching me so much and supporting me on this project. Finally, I would like to thank my godfather, Brother Ibo, who is no longer here but gave me so much love; your death was heart-breaking, but it gave me the courage and strength to finish writing this book, to accomplish my dream. I know you would have been proud of me.

CHAPTER 1

"AGH!" AKOSUA SCREAMED as she felt something cold and scaly grab her leg. She attempted to swim away from the tight unpleasant grasp. Unfortunately, she did not succeed and felt herself slowy being pulled under the cold water. Panic possessed her and she started to yell for her poor life, but sadly her friends were too far away on shore to hear her desperate and fearful cries.

She gave one last sorrowful and helpless glance at her peers' distant figures before the girl of seventeen dry seasons was fully yanked into the rayless ocean. Her high cheekbones twisted with terror, her ebony skin turned purple, and her thick curly kinky brown hair covered her face. Only the stars of the sky and the salt of the sea could hear her.

Akosua kicked profusely at the creature that kept pulling her deeper into the frigid water but its many tentacles grabbed her even tighter. The poor girl felt herself blanking out as a tremendous amount of water started to fill up her lungs. Terrified, she kicked out of desperation. Then she felt herself slipping into unconsciousness, slipping into a dark soundless room.

Akosua awoke and felt a warm presence that strangely enlightened her, but she was paralyzed by a murderous fear. After moments of fighting with her curiosity it won, and the girl of seventeen dry seasons opened her eyes.

"Don't be afraid my child," said a voice that sounded like music to her ears. It was sweet and harmonious.

Akosua blinked. She was agaped by both the sight in front of her and the being that the musical voice belonged to.

A mermaid floated in an enchanting room with tiny white shells glittering on intsensely blue walls. Akosua's body shook. She did not trust her brain.

The mermaid was the most magnificent thing Akosua had ever laid eyes upon. Her silky brown skin shone like gold, and her long brown enchanting locks flowed down her back and curled like the waves of the sea. Her stunning indigo tail swayed elegantly, and her smile was whiter than the whitest pearl. Akosua swore to herself that she saw waves in the mermaid's intense ebony eyes. The mermaid was the epitome of beauty. She was divine. Akosua was mesmerized and was unable to form a coherent phrase.

"I won't hurt you," said the mermaid with a gentle smile.

Her words reassured the astonished girl of seventeen dry seasons. However, many questions flooded Akosua's mind, and words poured out of her soul. "Are we in water? Why am I here? Who the heck are you? What did I do?"Akosua asked all at once.

The mermaid stayed quiet, listening, and then responded, this time with amusement in her voice, "Indeed, we are in water, in my palace to be exact."

Akosua swallowed. She wanted to believe it was just an insane dream but when a small blue and sliver striped fish brushed against her hand and she felt its coldness, the teen then knew it was all too real.

"I called for you. I asked one of my children to fetch you," the mermaid continued.

Akosua stared at the mermaid in utter disbelief. Anger started to fill her, "So you kidnapped me?" Akosua asked slowy, still trying to comprehend the baffling situation. "What are my friends going to think?" she added with sad desperation. A storm of rage and confusion started passing through the Akosua and the mermaid stayed quiet. The silence seemed to calm Akosua's emotional winds.

Finally, the mermaid spoke, "Let me explain my child."

"Why do you call me *my child*?!" Akosua exclaimed with irritation. Not caring if it would vex the mermaid, the teen mumbled a few insults to herself.

The mermaid kept a noble smile on her face and said softly, but with a great amount of force, "I'm Yemanja, goddess of all oceans and mother to all creatures of the seas, even earthlings."

Everything in the room shook, including Akosua. It sounded as if the most powerful waves were crashing against each other.

"I thought you were a myth," Akosua said quietly with awe and a mixture of confusion and disbelief. She suddenly felt so ashamed for being so rude.

"I am as real as you are," replied the goddess softly. "I called you *my child*, Akosua, because my oceans and my children are being killed and destroyed by the pollution humans create and cause."

Akosua gasped. This was the last thing she had expected the goddess to say, and she was even more unprepared for what the goddess would say next.

"I need you to warn humans that if they don't stop this chaos, they will have to pay terrible consequences," the goddess continued.

The teen almost choked out of disbelief, giggling nervously. "Haha this must be a joke," Akosua told the goddess, but when she saw that Yemanja's face was filled with seriousness, her heart almost fainted. "You want *me* to do what?" exclaimed Akosua. "But I'm just just a girl of seventeen dry seasons, I still don't know much of the world. I'm not rich. How would I travel? I literally get 15 Bajan dollars a month as an allowance."

After the teen had finished her rant, the goddess spoke softly with much eloquence and grace. "Enough my child. The stars of the sky and your ancestors who died crossing the Atlantic chose you. The ocean chose you. I chose you," Yemanja told the distressed teen.

Akosua was more silent than death. She tried to take everything in, but it was all too much. "What happens if I don't agree to this?" Akosua asked, breaking the deafening silence.

"Then you don't fulfill your destiny and will live your after life just wandering in chaos. Never knowing peace, just restlessness."

Akosua covered her face with her hands. She took a long breath, still confused as to how she was able to breathe under water. "When do I start?" Akosua asked bitterly.

"Soon. In two weeks." Yemanja inched forward and said, "I will send someone to accompany you and guide you. You don't need to worry about transportation and money." Akosua gulped. She was still bewildered about the whole ordeal.

"Akosua, you must make a choice. You can either tell your family about the mission in hopes that they will believe you, or not tell them anything and let them think you are dead or have run away," Yemanja explained to the teen with no hint of wit.

"This is so unfair," Akosua whispered with acrimony. She felt heart-broken. How would her family ever recover if they thought she was dead or had run away, and would they believe her if she told them the truth?

She sank her head into her chest, and thick tears threatened to pour down her cheeks. She deeply resented what she would say. "They won't believe me if I tell them the truth," she said in a feeble voice, barely audible.

The goddess stayed silent, then said, "Ok, it's settled then my child. You will leave in two weeks to warn the mundanes. You will travel the seven continents to carry out this important mission, but remember that your ancestors from great Africa give you their protection."

Akosua nodded solemnly and asked, "How will I convince humans? Why would they listen to a girl of seventeen dry seasons?"

"Faith is how," Yemanja simply responded.

This wasn't the answer Akosua wanted to hear. "Can I go home now?" she asked.

"You can. In two weeks, return to the beach and look out into the ocean. Chant my name three times. You have my blessing," said the goddess.

"Ok," Akosua said. She was drowning in her thoughts, still perplexed by how she was able to breathe under water. The goddess chanted some words and Akosua felt herself being hurled by waves.

"You have my blessing my child," Akosua heard the goddess Yemanja repeat.

Akosua felt herself emerge from the chilly water. She could hear her friends' worried voices calling out her name from the shore. Akosua swam toward the beach and got out of the ocean, the fresh cool air hitting her soft skin. She tried to reflect on all that had just happened, but her priority was to calm down her agitated and anxious friends. "I'm here guys," Akosua called to her two friends, Beeny and Lettaya, who were about to climb a coconut tree to get a better view of the ocean. This was ironic Akosua thought to herself. It was night and the ocean was mosaic black.

Lettaya almost fainted out of relief, and Beeny nearly fell off the coconut tree when they caught sight of their lost friend. They quickly sprinted to a wet and confused Akosua. "Oh, my goodness!

We've been looking for you for an hour. Where on earth did you go?" exclaimed Beeny who enveloped Akosua in a hug.

Lettaya, who was standing just behind Beeny, was in tears. "I could not have lived with myself if I had to tell your mom I lost you in the ocean. No more of her delicious rice and beans," Lettaya said in between sobs.

Akosua laughed, trying to make the mood lighter. "It's not funny Ak. Where were you?" Beeny asked with a serious tone.

Akosua's guts dropped. She had to lie. "Well, I was waiting for you two to come in the water, but you were taking so long so I decided to swim alone. I did not realize how far I was but then the currents started pulling me," Akosua said and paused, "I had to fight to get out, it was such a struggle."

Beeny studied Akosua fixedly. "Hum, I don't believe that," she stated. Beeny was clever and knew when Akosua was lying but did not utter another word. Her dark brown eyes surveyed Akasowa as her chocolate skin glimmered and her kinky hair stood royally on her head.

"I'm just glad you are ok, let's go home before our mothers actually start worrying," Lettaya said with reassurance. She was compassionate and understanding, her caramel skin shone along with the moon and her long curly hair blew with the wind.

The walk back was one of silence, not awkward but peaceful and right. The stars shone in the sky deep in conversation with the moon. The Barbados air was cool and fresh. It would be a moment Akosua would miss dearly. As the three girls approached Akosua's home, a typical Caribbean house, one of bright oranges,earthly reds, and lemony yellows. She suddenly announced to her friends, "I'm sorry about worrying you, but you know I love you guys, right?"

"We know," Beeny and Lettaya said in unison. They each gave her a kiss on the cheek and disappeared down the narrow road becoming one with the night.

CHAPTER 2

DOMINOS FORCEFULLY HITTING wood sounded in the background. The wind danced with the sweet melodic rhythm of soca. The crickets owned the night, singing in low raspy voices to the moon. Akosua lay on her bed and stared through her open window, looking up at the stars that embellished the sky. She was lost in a cloud of thoughts and consumed with worry.

A knock sounded on her door. "Akosua, may I come in?" asked a gentle voice.

It was Ina, Akosua's little sister. "You may," Akosua replied calmy, trying to keep her worry afar. Ina looked exactly like her older sister, except that she had a large scar across her forehead and was slighty shorter.

"You've been really silent these last couple of days. It's like you changed since you came back from the beach the other night," Ina remarked. "Your friends were frightened for you."

Akosua winced at the thought of the two weeks prior, when she had come back from Yemanja's palace and had been assigned with a lifechanging mission. She had disappeared for an hour and had worried her friends to death. She had promised herself that she would not tell her family or friends the truth because she feared they would not believe her. "I'm just reflecting on life, that's all," Akosua told her little sister after a long period of silence.

"I saw them at Mama Lo's shop the other day. They still seemed real paranoid about you disappearing. Why did you do that to them?" Ina asked.

"For the last time a bad current took me away," Akosua snapped, a bit irritated with her sister's question.

"Hum, you know it's extremely rare for someone to get out of a current. I'm glad you're ok," Ina told her sister with good intent.

Akosua sighed and grabbed her little sister's hand. She pulled her onto the wooden bed and tickled her. Ina, a girl of fourteen dry seasosns burst out laughing. The girl of seventeen dry seasons watched her beloved sister's face light up with joy and her heart sank. She would miss those precious tender moments. After regaining herself, Ina sat up and smiled at her older sister. "Laughing feels so good," the girl of fourteen dry seasons said happily.

Akosua nodded and replied, "It's healing." She rubbed her palm against the huge scar on her sister's forehead. Ina looked surprised but did not utter a word. "Remember how you got this wound?" Akosua asked her perplexed younger sister.

"Of course, I was little, maybe about four or five, and it was the end of mango season but there was one last ripe juicy mango in the tree near Auntie Mana's house. It was hanging on the highest branch and I told all the kids that I would get it and eat it," Ina breathed and continued, "They all laughed at me and told me I would never get it." Ina closed her eyes but kept talking, "I was stubborn and did not listen to them and I climbed the tree and fell. The kids all died with laughter."

"How did you feel?" asked Akosua.

Ina smiled slyly but replied, "I was honestly humiliated, but I still had faith and so what did I do? I climbed the tree again and this time I came back with a mango." She smiled brightly and widely, and said with pride, "Let me tell you, it was the best mango that I have ever tasted in my entire life. The other kids were burning with envy." Both of the girls laughed a sweet and tender laugh. Akosua needed to hear that story. It was a way of giving her confidence about the journey she would embark on in the morning. "Why did you ask to hear the story?" Ina asked with curiosity filling her voice.

"Your story shows that in life sometimes you must fall before you succeed," Akosua told her sister.

"Ohh, how profound," Ina said sarcastically. The girl of fourteen dry seasons got up and headed to the door. "Gotta go help Ma with dinner, I promised her," she told her older sister. Ina slipped out of the room.

Once again Akosua was lost in the midst of her thoughts. She reflected on the journey around the world that she would be embarking on in the morning. She had not uttered one word about the whole ordeal to anyone. The girl of seventeen dry seasons would just disappear. Akosua felt a deep sense of guilt and knew it would pain her mother and all her loved ones, but she was a chosen one. She grabbed her half-broken smart phone and texted her two friends, Beeny and Lettaya.

She wrote three sentences:

> *The ocean needs me.*
> *My love for you girls remains strong.*
> *I'm sorry.*

Rain poured out of Akosua's eyes and her heart thundered. She was not ready for the tough roads ahead of her, and the thought of never seeing her friends and family again saddened her tremendously. She sighed, wiped her tears, and put on a mask (a fake smile and an expressionless stare). The girl of seventeen dry seasons went downstairs and spent the night dancing, eating, laughing and talking to her family, pretenting everything was normal, but she continued to wear the mask.

Her family was totally oblivious to her emotions and her departure at sunrise.

The day was still young. Roosters held their heads high as they sang to the sun. Mothers were in their kitchens, cooking breakfast to break their familes' night fast. Children's eyes were red from somber. They slowy got out of bed, lost between two worlds, dreams and reality. Men put on their work clothes, the clicking of the pans in the kitchen was their alarm. Akosua rushed around in her room, grabbing anything that seemed useful to her and forcing it in a suitcase that was passé, but that was the least of her worries. She had to find a way to get out of the house without being noticed by her family.

She could hear her relatives' buoyant voices downstairs and for a moment, she was tempted to say goodbye, but she knew she could not. Akosua gripped her suitcase tightly, placed her handbag on her shoulder and put a big straw hat on her head. She took one last sullen glance at her room. She let her eyes pause at the pictures of her loved ones on the wall and at all the surf medals she had won. Then, she jumped out her bedroom window. Luckily for her, it was not a far jump. She fell, but quickly got up and started running toward the beach.

There were locals walking their cows or on their way to the market who greeted her, "Hello Akosua," some said. Akosua acknowledged them, but before they had a chance to respond and ask where she was rushing off to, Akosua had already sprinted far away, her mahogony slik dress dancing with the wind.

The turquoise waves were crashing onto the shore when Akosua arrived. The beach was empty, inhabited only by tall coconut trees and the pretty beige sand. She breathed, looked out into the vast ocean, and chanted three times as she was told, "Yemanja. Yemanja. Yemanja." She waited, and became a bit impatient when nothing seemed to happen. She watched families of waves wash up on the shore, bringing shells with them, and then taking them back.

An eternity seemed to pass until a huge wave came and a beautiful young woman emerged from the water. She had thick brown locks with cowrie shells hanging at the end of one. The woman was elegant, and pride was written all over her face as she walked out of the ocean without a single drop of water on her body. The young woman approached Akosua, her eyes twinkling and her white lace dress fitting perfectly to the curves of her body. It was as if someone took all the stars in the sky and placed them in the woman's eyes. Akosua stared.

"I'm Emaye, daughter of Yemanja. I will guide you throughout your journey," the young woman said with a kind smile. She had an interesting voice, Akosua thought to herself It was powerful, yet gentle.

"Nice to meet you, I'm just Akosua," the adolescent said with a hint of shyness in her voice.

Emaye laughed a hearty laugh. Akosua barely knew the mysterious woman who emerged from the ocean but she already liked her. Emaye looked out at the ocean as if it was talking to her. She nodded her head to it. "Your ancestors who crossed the Atlantic during the European slave trade send you their protection and wish us a safe and victorious journey," Emaye informed the girl of seventeen dry seasons.

"They told you?" Akosua asked, stunned.

Emaye nodded. "They are the waves of the sea," she said with no surprise in her voice. "Of course they did." The girl of seventeen dry seasons nodded as if she understood, but she was completely confused. "We must hurry if we want to catch our flight," Emaye said, breaking Akosua's chain of thought.

"Oh, right, where are we going first?" Akosua asked, feeling overwhelmed by the thought of what awaited her. She was just relieved to have someone accompany her.

"I will tell you all at the airport," the young woman said. Akosua nodded, not in a mood to protest, but still wondering how they would get there. "Come here Akosua," Emaye said gently. Emaye stood by the shore, her feet in the water, holding a beautiful pink sea shell. "Place your finger on the shell and think of something positive or something that makes you happy," Emaye told a perplexed Akosua.

The girls of seventeen dry seasons was hesitant but placed her little finger on the shell. She tried to think of something positive but was torn. Her thoughts were sad ones, about leaving her family behind. Emaye studied Akosua and saw her struggling, "Close, your eyes, sweet one, and breathe. Think of laughing with someone you love."

It worked. Akosua smiled at the thought of her little sister's laugh. One of pure joy and love. Suddenly, Akosua felt herself being transported by the air. Her body spun, and her finger never left the shell. She saw Emaye's face, but it was blurry. She saw flashes of white and indigo blue. Finally, everything came to a stop and she felt a hand grasp her by the shoulder. "Akosua, get up." She heard Emaye's powerful, gentle voice in the distance and her eyes flew open. Akosua wore a perplexed expression on her face when she realized that she was sitting in the middle of the airport on a cold, shiny, gray marble floor.

Passersby glanced down at her as if she had two huge horns sticking out of her head. She quickly got up and rushed toward Emaye who was a few feet away looking for something in a brown bag that Akosua just noticed. "Did we just teleport? Oh, my God, please tell me I'm dreaming," she sputtered.

Amusement glimmered behind the pupils of Emaye's dark brown eyes, "It's not a dream, now follow me," she told Akosua truthfully. Akosua said no more and followed Emaye to the check–in desk. Emaye walked so elegantly that many people stopped in their tracks to admire her grace and beauty. It was as if she put them in a trance.

"Hello," a woman with bright red lipstick and a thick bun greeted them at the desk, "How can I help you?"

"Hi, we are on flight 17936 going to England. Our final destination is Beijing, China," Emaye responded to the lady.

"May I have your names please," the lady asked Emaye.

Akosua kept looking around nervously, hoping no one would recognize her. Barbados was a small island and word got around fast. Emaye stated their names and Akosua was surprised that Emaye knew her last name. She promised herself that she would ask Emaye about it.

"I can't find you in our system," the lady told the two travelers in an irritated manner.

"Check again. We are on the list." The lady wanted to protest but Emaye's voice washed over her like the waves of the ocean. The lady looked confused and dazed but stared closely at her computer.

"Oh, I'm sorry, I found you ladies," the lady announced. She clicked the screen and printed out two tickets. Akosua's eyes widened as Emaye thanked the woman and took the tickets.

"Our names were not on that list. How did you make her do that?" Akosua asked Emaye as they walked away from the desk.

"I hope you took everything you needed with you," Emaye said to Akosua ignoring her question.

Akosua started to get irritated by not getting answers. "Will you tell me how?" she demanded.

"Later," Emaye said vaguely. She walked toward security and an irritated Akosua followed, still glancing around worriedly.

"You should stop. It will only make you paranoid," Emaye told the girl of seventeen dry seasons.

Akosua opened her little mouth to protest, but instead remained silent in fear of causing a commotion that would attract attention. They breezed through security and walked straight to their gate. It was a short walk since the airport in Barbados was not very big. Once at the gate, familes sat talking, tourists looked stressed, and other individuals read books or looked at their smart phones. That's it, the teen thought. It was the start of her journey.

"Let's sit," Emaye said to the nervous teen. Akosua nodded and followed her to the nearest row of empty seats.

Akosua suddenly felt her heart drop, "I don't think I can do this Emaye," she exclaimed with panic.

"Come on, sit," Emaye said as she directed Akosua to an open seat. Pain was written all over Akosua's face and thick tears reddened her eyes. Emaye's eyes filled with pity but when she spoke, it sounded like the waves of the sea again. "Listen, it takes much sorrow and sacrifices to attain the greatest results. You are fulfilling your destiny and inscribing yourself in eternity. Akosua, you are the pillar of this mission. If you fail then everything will crumble with you. Now wipe your tears, salt water dries human skin." Akosua sniffed, took the napkin Emaye handed her and wiped away her tears but not the redness they left behind. That would stay.

"We are now boarding flight 17936," an announcer's voice sounded.

The young woman and the girl of seventeen dry seasons slowly got up. They grabbed their belongings, adjusted their dresses and moved onto the frigid aircraft. She had not even left the island, but Akosua already longed and craved for her return.

The forest green landscape blurred as the plane flew farther into the grayish and partly cloudy sky. This time, it was Akosua's heart that cried. She was leaving her beautiful beloved island behind. Her head was pressed against the window as she watched Emaye's hands fidget.

"Are you afraid of planes?" Akosua asked, a bit amused by the thought of Emaye being scared of something.

Emaye turned and looked at Akosua. "Let's just say, I prefer the ocean," the young woman said shaking nervously.

"You, the strong fierce Emaye, are afraid of planes? Unbelievable," Akosua said and erupted in giggles. Emaye frowned and opened her mouth to respond, but the airplane started to move agitatedly. The young woman forcefully shut her eyes and planted her hand in Akosua's. The teen could not stop laughing, and said to Emaye who by then, had her face buried in her hand, "It's just turbulence. It's normal." The young woman did not budge. She was paralyzed with terror. "You seem so fearless, I would have never expected this in a million years," Akosua commented after she had stopped laughing.

"Well, everyone is afraid of something, we all have our weaknesses," Emaye said, her voiced muffled by her hands.

"Touche," the girl of seventeen dry seasons said with a slight smirk on her face.

The flight to England seemed like an eternity to Akosua. The turbulence got bored and went away. Emaye, who had been sitting for hours with her hands covering her face, seemed to relax and came out from hiding.

CHAPTER 3

"It's cold," Akosua complained to Emaye, "I thought we were going straight to the hotel." China's cold, and thick air hit against her silky skin as they walked the large streets of Bejing. The buildings rose high and the architecture was one that the Bajan had never seen before.

"This is not vacation, Akosua. This is a serious mission. We have to vist a friend of mine first," Emaye reminded Akosua. The girl of seventeen dry seasons felt a little ashamed and stayed quiet.

People in the streets pulled out their phones and took pictures of them. It deeply disturbed Akosua to the point that she was on the verge of insulting an older Chinese man. Emaye noticed her uneasiness. "Don't mind them. They have never seen blacks before," she told the distraught Akosua.

"I figured, but I just don't like feeling as if I'm some wild animal in the zoo," Akosua exclaimed.

"I totally understand," Emaye simply responded, "It isn't pleasant."

"How do you know all these things Emaye? Do you travel a lot?" Akosua asked curiously, realizing that she did not know much about Emaye.

Emaye grinned and took a slow breath and then said, "Traveling is vital for my health, I love it and need it. Sadly, I can't always travel."

Feeling comfortable, Akosua asked more questions, "Where are you from? Also, what are you? You just emerged from the water without one single drop of water on your body when I met you."

Emaye laughed. "Man, you sure do ask a lot of questions," she said with good heart, "But that's a good thing sometimes."

"I have just traveled half way across the world with you and don't know much about you," Akosua said with a sly smile on her face, "I need to know about who I'm dealing with."

"Fair enough,"Emaye said with a laugh, "I'm Yemanja's daughter and I live and work at one of her palaces on the coast of Brazil."

"Wait, so you are a fish?" Akosua questioned, a bit stunned.

Emaye shook her head, "I have the abilty to breathe underwater, so I'm kinda like a mermaid with no tail, but I have the power to live on land as a human being as well," she said. "I collect the offerings that the Afro Brazillians put in the ocean for Yemanja," Emaye added.

"They believe in Yemanja in Brazil?" Akosua asked with more surprise.

"Of course. She plays a major part in their religion, Candomble," Emaye said with pride. "In Haiti, Cuba, and other parts of the

Americas and Africa, of course, you can find Yemanja. She has different names but is fundamentally the same."

Akosua's eyes filled with awe. "Wow," the teen whispered.

"Akosua, Yemanja told me that you knew who she was," Emaye told the amazed adolescent.

"Yea, actually I did. There used to be a Nigerian man, Pa Shango, who would tell the children of the neighborhood stories about the African divinities. He would always mention Yemanja,"Akosua explained, "I think because he had a special affinity with her or something."

Akosua sighed and said softly, "I thought all those stories were all myths."

Emaye smiled slyly and turned down a narrow obscure street. "Are you sure that this is the way?" Akosua asked, hesitant about following Emaye down the dark street.

"Positive,"Emaye replied, not stopping and looking back at her dubious traveling companion,

"I really don't want to get jumped by a panda bear, Emaye," Akosua warned.

Emaye burst out laughing and, after catching her breath, said "You have a lot of imagination, Akosua."

"It's not funny fish girl," Akosua responded, erupting into fits of giggles.

Emaye pretended to look hurt and continued to walk. She stopped abruptly in front of a beautiful sturdy brown door. "This is it," she announced. Emaye put down her bag, knocked on the door and waited. A tall young man with silky, rich, brown skin and dark, gentle, mysterious eyes, and high cheek bones, opened the door. He gave them a bright smile and said in an orotund voice "Emaye, oh Emaye." He motioned for Emaye and Akosua to enter. The home was vibrant and warm with beautiful Ethiopian paintings hanging on the orange walls and photographs of tropical scenery sitting in frames. It was welcoming and Akosua felt the void in her heart heal a little.

"Ayele, it's been so long," Emaye said as she and the man hugged.

"It has my dear," the man said sweetly. He then turned to Akosua. "Hello, I'm Ayele," he said, stretching out his hand to Akosua.

She shook it and kindly smiled. "I'm Akosua. This is a lovely home," she told Ayele.

"Ayele is from Ethiopia," Emaye interrupted before Ayele could respond.

"Wow, what brought you to China?" Akosua asked Ayele, both amazed and surprised.

The young man gave a handsome grin, "I've always been an adventuer." He added, "In Africa, the Chinese have come and started to set up their shops and sell cheap plastic products to the locals. These products pollute Africa and many African businesses start to go bankrupt. That's why I made it my mission to live in China to try to convince them to stop creating these cheap products to sell not only in Africa but the rest of the world," Ayele finished with passion.

"And how have they reacted?" Akosua asked, hopeful.

"There is a lot of racism here, I get called monkey sometimes," he replied.

The teen's heart sank. How would she, a girl of seventeen dry seasons and a native of Barbados, convince the Chinese to stop polluting the oceans?

"But I shall never give up," Ayele continued with exuberance and pride.

Akosua barely knew the man, but she respected him.

Emaye smiled softly and said, "Ayele, Akosua has been chosen with the mission of the oceans."

Ayele looked surprised but quickly hid it and simply said, "It is an honor to be in your presence." Akosua smiled in response and watched Ayele look at Emaye questionably.

"I will make some tea, may I, Ayele?" Emaye said walking into his kitchen.

"Of course, let me help," he replied and turned to Akosua. "You are at home. Please sit wherever you'd like." He pointed at a sofa and a couple of wooden chairs. Akosua sat down on the fluffy, red sofa. She was tired. She could hear Emaye and Ayele whispering in the kitchen and gulped. Akosua was convinced that they knew something she did not, and it made her uneasy.

She let her eyes wander and they settled on a pretty photograph of an extremely beautiful beach. It resembled so much the one in Barbados. Her heart started to ache at the thought of her island. The thought of her family lingered with her. "It's beautiful, isn't it?"

Ayele said from across the room, his strong melodic voice resonating in Akosua's ears. He watched her stare at the picture.

She nodded and said, "It reminds me of my home, Barbados."

Ayele could see the pain and distress on Akosua's face when she mentioned her island. "I heard it's a beautiful island, but I took this picture in Karukera," he explained.

"Oh, you're a photographer?" the adolescent asked, curiosity pushing her pain away.

The young Ethiopian man smiled and said, "It's one of my passions." He had a pretty set of white teeth.

"Wow, that's awesome. I've never heard of Karukera before but from your picture it is magnificent," Akosua told Ayele.

He studied the photo, "It really is, but today due to colonization, it is known as Guadeloupe. Karukera was the original name given by the indigenous people. It means "Island of beautiful waters,"Ayele explained with eloquence. Akosua closed her eyes and tears poured out of them. She was tired and still very sensitive. As a result, talking about islands made her heart swell. It reminded her of home and what she had to leave behind.

Noticing Akosua's distress, Ayele said gently and with a well of compassion in his voice, "Hey, when you are in exile or far from home, you miss your family and country deeply. There will be days you long to feel the sun against your skin and talk to people, but you must adapt. The return home will be all the sweeter."

Heat spread throughout Akosua's face. She nodded and wiped away her tears as fast as she could, a bit embarrassed, because she was crying in a man's house that she barely knew. Emaye emerged from the kitchen holding a small silver tray and three elegant Chinese tea cups. "Tea everyone?" Emaye asked, as she placed the tray on the coffee table. Emaye sat beside Akosua on the sofa, and Ayele sat across from them on a brown chair.

"Ayele has agreed to help us get a meeting with the Chinese government," Emaye told Akosua as she sipped her tea.

"I have contacts," a smiling Ayele added.

Akosua sighed, "That's a relief. I was wondering how I would talk to them."

They all sipped quitetly on their tea until Akosua broke the silence with her humming. She tended to do that when she was nervous or anxious. "Tomorrow, I think we should talk to the officals," Emaye told the teen interrupting her humming. Akosua nodded, anxiety filling up her insides. Ayele and Emaye started talking but Akosua blanked out. The jet lag was catching up with her. She let herself yawn. The tiredness had won.

"We should go. Thanks for everything Ayele," Emaye said as she looked at the exhausted girl of seventeen dry seasons, who was on the verge of falling asleep on the sofa. "Akosua," Emaye called gently and the girl jumped up. She was a little dazed. "Come back to earth," Emaye said, making her and Ayele erupt in laughter.

"Oh!" Akosua said with a sheepish expression, "Sorry."

Emaye and Akosua hugged Ayele and thanked him for everything. Then they slowy and peacefully left his house. Once they were outside and back on the busy streets of Bejing, Akosua commented,

"He's really nice." Emaye nodded with assent. "Mind if I ask you how you how know him?" she pried.

"Wow, you are suddenly not tired anymore," Emaye replied with a smug smirk on her face. Akosua rolled her eyes, but Emaye continued, "I don't know if Ayele mentioned that he is a professional photographer, but seven years ago I needed someone to take pictures of a ceremony for Yemanja and he happened to be available. We have been friends ever since."

Akosua nodded, "That's really cool," she replied.

The city lights shone brightly, and Akosua could not believe that she was in China. She wanted to inhale the air but was terrified of the pollution that would infiltrate her lungs. "Is the hotel far?"she asked tiredly, suddenly noticing the weight of the bags on her shoulder.

"I honestly don't know. Let us take a taxi," Emaye finally said with nonchalance after looking at the street names."

"Emaye! You said it was five minutes away,"Akosua exclaimed, but Emaye ignored her impatient tone and hailed a cab and they climbed in. Lucklily the driver spoke a little English and Emaye was able to explain to him where the hotel was. Akosua looked at Emaye sprawled across the car seat. She suddenly looked pale and sullen."Emaye, are you ok?"Akosua asked worriedly.

"I'll be ok, just bring my bags up to the hotel and give this to the driver," Emaye answered in an extremely feeble voice as she handed Akosua some Renminbi bills with shaky frail hands. After a few minutes, the cab stopped abruptly in front of a decent hotel.

It wasn't the nicest looking one. Emaye rushed out and struggled to climb the many stairs toward the hotel's entrance.

Akosua gave the driver the money, thanked him, and grabbed all the bags before carefully making her way up the many stairs. By the time the overloaded girl of seventeen dry seasons arrived in the hotel's grand lobby, Emaye had the room keys. She looked even more ghostly. "Let's go to the hotel room," Emaye said, her voice weak and faint.

"Emaye, what's wrong?"Akosua asked. She was extremely worried, but Emaye just made a hand gesture for her to follow. Emaye limped into the hotel room. "Oh, my God. I need to get you help!" Akosua exclaimed with panic.

"No, please," Emaye pleaded. Akosua took her hand and guided her to the nearest bed to sit. "I have salt in my bag, grab it, and fill the bath tub with water," Emaye instructed in a voice so feeble that Akosua could barely hear.

"How is that going to help you?"asked Akosua.

"Trust me. Please, do it quickly," Emaye whispered.

Akosua did as she was told. She rushed into the bathroom and filled the tub with water. Then she grabbed a silk bag filled with salt from Emaye's bag and handed it to her. Again, she helped Emaye up and led her toward the bathroom. Once Emaye entered, she closed the door behind her, separating herself from the exhausted and worried girl of seventeen dry seasons. Akosua waited for hours and forced herself to stay awake until finally, a rejuvenarated, smiling, and glowing Emaye emerged from the bathroom. Akosua gasped in shock She could not believe her eyes. "You should have slept," Emaye told her.

"How could I? You looked so sick," Akosua said after studying Emaye intensely.

"I see you care for me," Emaye giggled.

Akosua rolled her eyes a bit annoyed and said, "It's called being a human being. But seriously, can you explain to me what the heck happened? Why do you look so well?"

"What? I can't look good?" Emaye replied with a smirk, avoiding Akosua's question.

"Fine, don't tell me anything."Akosua said, as anger rose in her voice. The teenager jumped under the bed's blankets and covered her head with a huge white pillow.

Emaye saw that Akosua was upset. "I'll tell you in the morning, ok?" she told the angry teen.

"Don't bother, I want to know now!"Akosua exclaimed, her voice muffled by the pillow.

Emaye sighed reluctantly and said, "Alright, I'll tell you." Akosua bolted from underneath the covers. Her thick brown hair was pushed to one side of her head and her eyes were red from fatigue. "Why did I become weak and pale?" Emaye repeated Akosua's question.

Akosua nodded her head. "Yes, explain," she insisted.

"You are probably also wondering why I could not go on this mission on my own?" Emaye asked.

"Actually, it did cross my mind,"Akosua admitted.

"I could not go on this mission on my own because I was not

chosen. You were." Emaye paused before continuing, "And the reason I got ill is because I'm Yemanja's daughter and if people don't believe in her or that the ocean has a spirit, then they don't believe in me, which means I can't be seen." The room was silent. "As a result, I sometimes have to use my powers to be seen but it can be physically and mentally exhausting, and it can make me ill if I use them too much." Once again, Akosua was at a loss for words, so she just listened. "If I don't use my powers, I will be invisible or a shadow to many. I'm sorry Akosua, but I can't be in the meeting with you tomorrow, I need to restore my powers," Emaye informed the teen calmly.

Akosua sank, "What! Maybe the people at the meeting believe in Yemanja, I need you," she said desperately, but Emaye wore a saddened expression on her face.

"I doubt it my dear," she told her, "Akosua, don't stress, you will do fine."

Akosua stayed quiet for a moment then asked, "How come I see you then?"

"You see me because you believe in Yemanja or that the ocean has a spirit," Emaye responded gently. "Humans make Yemanja real. If people did not believe in her, she would not exist."

Akosua shook her head, tryng to wrap her brain around the new information. "This is a lot to take in. Emaye, what will I even say in the meeting tomorrow? I will make a fool of myself," she said in a sorrowful tone.

"I know it is hard, but let me show you something," Emaye told her. She took Akosua's hand and mumbled a few words. "Close your eyes," Akosua heard Emaye say. She did as she was told but did not expect what awaited her. She felt pain jab at her heart when she saw millions of pieces of plastic in the ocean. Hundreds of thousands of fish and sea creatures were either stuck in it or eating it. She saw millions of fish lying on their backs dead, and enormous tsunamis rushing towards land. She saw millions of people lying dead, their breaths stolen, limbs hanging on trees and roosters now quiet. It was a disaster of an unimagined magnitude.

Akosua's eyes shot open. "Oh, my God!" she exlcaimed, feeling heartbroken and distressed. "That was awful. We have to do something, Emaye. We will die if we don't," she cried.

"You can do something," Emaye told her in a serious tone. Akosua felt devastated, she knew that she would try her best to stop the chaos from occurring, but how would she do it? She had no clue. "Tomorrow, go into the meeting using your heart and soul," Emaye told Akosua. "No sugar coating, just the honest and raw truth."

CHAPTER 4

A BLACK GIRL of seventeen dry seasons moved throughout the city of Beijing as if she had lived there her entire life. However, the truth was that Akosua had never set foot in China, and certainly not Beijing. In fact, she was being guided by Emaye who was invisible to many so that she could preserve her powers. "I'm nervous," Akosua told Emaye who was walking fast while her locks and red cotton dress danced with the wind. The teen wore a simple but elegant brown lace dress with pretty seashell earrings.

"Don't be. Oh, there is Ayele," Emaye said, and pointed to a smiling Ayele walking toward them.

Akosua and Emaye embraced Ayele in a warm and loving hug. "It's good to see you this morning," he told them sweetly. Akosua smiled and Emaye said a bit briskly, "We should get going."

Ayele looked down at the silver watch he was wearing. "Right, follow me," he said. They did so without protest. Many people stared at them as they walked by.

"They have probably never seen three black people at the same time," Akosua caught herself saying, "Oh, I mean, *two* black people at the same time. They probably don't believe in Yemanja," Akosua corrected herself.

Ayele eyed Emaye curiously at Akosua's correction. "I told her," Emaye told Ayele bluntly.

He smiled and looked at Akosua, "How did you take it?"

"I was shocked, to be honest." Akosua answered with a laugh. Ayele joined in. It was the type of laugher that made worries disappear.

"I understand, I almost had a heart attack myself when I found out," Ayele finally told Akosua when they were done laughing their hearts out.

Emaye swatted Ayele on the arm. "Oh, shush Ayele, you are too dramatic," she scolded him in amusement. They all erupted in sweet laughter and Akosua, who had been feeling nervous all morning about her meeting, started to relax. They arrived in front of an all white building with a surprisingly huge sign that read *Enviromentalist*.

"We are here. You will be talking to some environmentalists today as you can see," Ayele said to Akosua as he pointed to the sign. "Emaye and I can't come in with you but go in and state your name at the desk."

Akosua nodded and mumbled, "Thank you."

Emaye hugged her and whispered, "Just be honest."

Akosua gulped. She waved to Ayele and Emaye and slowly made

her way to the entrance. She took a deep breath before pushing through the building's door. Inside pretty Chinese paintings hung on the walls and the floor was shiny black marble. Akosua made her way to the desk where a Chinese woman sat. "Hello," Akosua said, afraid that the woman would not understand. To her surprise, the woman responded in perfect English.

"How can I help you?"

A little startled, Akosua took a while to reply, "Um, yes, I am Akosua. I have a meeting at 10 am," she told the lady.

"Ok, sit and I will call you," the woman instructed Akosua and pointed to a row of uncomfortable looking black leather seats. She waited fifteen minutes before the lady at the desk directed her to a room at the end of the hallway. Akosua knocked before entering. The room was small but spacious at the same time. There was a wooden table and a couple of chairs where a Chinese woman and man sat. Their hair was darker than midnight, and their oval shaped eyes stared Akosua up and down. The teen kindly greeted them, and they said something to each other in Mandarin and burst out laughing. Akosua's face burned with embarrassment.

"You look so young," the man said to Akosua.

Emaye had told her to be honest, and that was exactly what she did. "I'm seventeen dry seasons actually."

The man and woman erupted in a mocking laughter. Akosua tried to keep her cool and took a seat facing them. "I've come with a message," Akosua said with authority after their laughter died out. However, by this time, the Chinese woman had pulled out her phone and was texting while the man's eyes were on the verge of shutting. "How disrespectful!" Akosua exclaimed. "I flew all the way from Barbados. I left my friends and family behind just to be here today," Akosua stated, anger filling her voice, "And you can't even give me one minute of your attention?"

The Chinese woman and man were agaped. The woman dropped her phone and the man's eyes were bulging out of his skull. Akosua had gotten their attention. They were listening. "Now, that I've gotten your attention, I will say what I've come here for,"Akosua told them. She paused before continuing, "Humans are polluting the oceans and millions of fish are dying. If we continue to pollute, we will die as well because the ocean produces a great amount of oxygen. We need to stop creating toxic substances or cut down on them because they end up poisoning the ocean."

Akosua kept her eyes on the woman and man to see if they were listening. They were indeed listening, so she continued. "Do you want your children and your children's children to have to suffer for what we are doing to the ocean?" Akosua was eloquent and passionate, and lectured for another twenty minutes. She was a natural, and when she had finished, the woman and man got up and shook her hand, thanking her. They also promised that they would bring the matter up with the officials of China. Akosua left them the card Emaye had instructed her to give to them, and the woman and man told her they would be in touch.

Akosua rushed out of the building with a huge smile embellishing her face. Emaye and Ayele were waiting for her where she had left them. Emaye proudly smiled back at Akosua. "From the smile on your face, I take it that it went well," Emaye said to Akosua. The delighted teen nodded and explained to them what happened.

"You showed them," Ayele said laughing and giving Akosua a fist bump. "Can I take you lovely ladies out to eat? This occasion calls for celebration!" Akosua beamed with pride.

"Yea, let's celebrate," Emaye said with a grin, "Akosua deserves it."

'So, what's next?"Akosua asked Emaye. They were seated in a Congolese restaurant. Pictures of Patrice Lumumba covered the walls and the famous singer, Aurlus Mabele, blasted loudly from the speakers. It had been an unexpected but pleasant surprise for Akosua.

"We have to see how the Chinese government responds or Yemanja might have to send out warnings," Emaye answered the teen frankly.

"What type of warnings?" Akosua asked, her voice quiet and a little timid.

"I don't know. It's her who decides," Emaye simply replied.

"So where are you guys heading next? Are you staying in Asia?" Ayele asked while eating a hand full of fufu.

"Logically, it would make sense if we stayed in Asia but Yemanja does not think so," Emaye told them.

The young woman seemed to know everything and Akosua was amazed by her wisdom.

"Then, where are we off too?" Akosua asked, a bit confused.

"Don't worry, she'll inform me soon," Emaye peacefully told Akosua.

"So, how do you guys like the food?" Ayele asked, trying to change the subject.

"Well, it's interesting. Pretty good, but I just don't think I could eat this everyday,"Akosua told him as she bit into her fufu. They all giggled, finished their African meal, and spent the rest of the day exploring Beijing. Akosua felt better than she had in days. She still missed her family to death, but her new friends made it more manageable. The void in her heart started to fill up a little and the girl of seventeen dry seasons felt less helpless and alone.

Akosua felt like crying. She and Emaye were at the airport saying goodbye to Ayele. Akosua had only known him for a couple of days but had gotten very attached to him. Ayele had helped Akosua ease her pain. She noticed that leaving Ayele also saddened Emaye terribly, but she would not mention it until they were in private. "Are you sure you can't come?"Akosua asked for the fourth time that day.

"Alas, I wish I could, Akosua, but I have many things to finish here in China first," Ayele told her, as hurt stained his pupils. The three of them stood silently in the middle of the airport, enjoying and disliking this bittersweet moment all at the same time.

"We should go," Emaye finally said. She cleared her throat and blinked away tears. She had decided not to use her powers that day, so it would would appear to the man as if Akosua was traveling all alone. Akosua nodded sadly.She turned sorrowfully toward the young Ethiopian and embraced him tightly.

"Goodbye my little sister. I wish you courage on your journey," Ayele told Akosua lovingly.

"When will I see you again?" Akosua asked, not really expecting a response.

"When the gods want," Ayele said quietly but with power in his words. The young man turned toward Emaye and stared at her like she was the most beautiful thing on the surface of the earth. They hugged. It was tender and sweet and seemed to suggest that they were more than friends.

"Emaye. Akosua. Farewell." Ayele said gently. He bowed his head to them with respect and love and disappeared within a massive crowd, as quiet as a fox. Akosua felt the void again, eating at her.

"Come on sis," Emaye told Akosua, and they made their way toward security. No one stopped to ask for Emaye's passport since she could not be seen Hours later, when they were on the plane, and after Emaye had seemed to relax, Akosua asked her a question that had been feeding her curiosity for a while.

"Was Ayele your boyfriend?" She regretted it once she saw the sullen expression Emaye wore.

Emaye took a deep breath and attempted to remove the solemn look on her face, "More than that, Ayele and I were going to get married," Emaye admitted in a calm voice.

Akosua's head went blank, "Married?" She almost choked.

"Yes, but his parents had other plans for him." Emaye answered in a soft voice.

"What type of plans?" Akosua urged.

"Arranged marriage. He was introduced to a woman and at first he was against it. But his family insisted, and he started to like her,"

Emaye uttered. Her composure broke and a single tear rolled down her face.

"Oh, Emaye. I'm so very sorry," Akosua told the pained young woman, "I shouldn't have asked."

Emaye waved her hand to Akosua, "It's alright and don't be sorry, it was a while ago." Emaye wiped away her tear. The girls of seventeen dry seasons was certain that the conversation was terminated but, to her surprise, Emaye continued. "It was a hard time because I was emotionally attached and put so much of myself in our relationship. When Ayele started to like this woman, he also started to forget about me. I became weak spiritually and sometimes my body would even fade."

"I just can't believe that Ayele would do that to you. How could anybody forget you?" Akosua asked, struggling to find the words. She was shocked.

Emaye sighed, "It happens. I had to use some of my magic to separate myself emotionally from him. I was so sick that my mother gave me strength to heal myself too."

"Yemanja?" Akosua asked Emaye.

"Yes, I was so sick. I was on the verge of disappearing. It is extremely dangerous for Yemanja's children to fall in love with mundanes who have no conception of the gods."

Akosua was stunned, "How do you feel now?" she asked gently.

"I'm better, almost healed but not quite." Emaye told the concerned teen, "Ayele and I have remained friends, but Ayele still has feelings for me which makes it difficult at times."

"Could you please be quiet, you have been talking to yourself nearly the whole flight," an older man with white skin and cold blue eyes frowned at Akosua. The teen and the young woman erupted in laughter. Akosua looked like a mad girl laughing and talking to herself. "That's it! I 'm calling the flight attendant," the man announced to Akosua with an evil smirk on his face.

Akosua turned toward Emaye a bit worried and asked, "Um, Emaye, what do I do?"

Emaye smiled cunningly and simply said, "Just watch."

A Chinese flight attendant, dressed in a black and navy-blue uniform, arrived in first class and stood in front of the older white man. "Yes, sir, how may I assist you?" she asked him.

"Yes, the young woman over there sitting alone keeps talking to herself. She's a mad person," he informed the flight attendant while he pointed his long, crooked fingers at Akosua. The flight attendant looked over to Akosua and saw a smiling Akosua and a beaming Emaye next to her.

"Is there a problem?" Emaye asked the flight attendant.

"No, this can't be possible! The young woman has been sitting alone all the flight!" the man shouted. Emeya and Akosua smiled slyly. Once the flight attendant disappeared down the narrow isle, Akosua turned to the man with a big grin. He glared at her, his cold blue eyes cruel with rage. "You, mad people!" he exclaimed.

"Hush or you will be expelled out of this aircraft," Akosua said imitating the flight attendant.

Akosua and Emaye giggled. "That was nice magic you did but you should stop because it's draining you," Akosua told Emaye quietly but the young woman smiled.

"I really appreciate the concern but if I use my powers from time to time for short periods, I should be fine," Emaye said, grateful for Akosua's concern.

"I see that you got more comfortable with planes," Akosua said to Emaye, laughing gleefully.

Emaye smiled again and was on the verge of replying when the plane started shaking brutally. Turbulence had taken over. "Oh, God!" Emaye cried in alarm.

"It will be fine don't worry." Akosua tried to sooth the distressed young woman, but was not successful. As a result of being consumed by fear, Emaye's magic started to fade and she became invisible to the eyes of unbelievers. That was what Emaye called the people who did not believe in Yemanja or that the ocean had spirit. "It's gonna be alright," Akosua kept telling a terrified Emaye, who was clasped onto her arm, leaving marks on her rich brown skin. It hurt, but Akosua kept that to herself.

"I'm not a sky person, I belong with the sea," Emaye muttered over and over for hours until she rocked herself to sleep. When she woke, the sky was grey, threatening to pour its tears onto the earth.

"It's a little chilly," Akosua remarked. She was always the first to speak about the weather.

"Yea, London is usually like this," Emaye agreed.

"Hum, to say that the people on my island dream to come here," Akosua pondered as she looked around the gloomy city.

"The propaganda of the west is used to dislocate the races," Emaye simply said and Akosua understood exactly what she meant. She too used to dream of visiting London. She also dreamed of having the bluest eyes and the longest blonde hair. Akosua used to dislike her features, her ebony skin and her thick brown curly hair.

"London is pretty, but so overrated. I think I would rather see Africa or South America." Akosua sighed, then asked, "Why are we here again? You said we were not staying long."

'We are not, we've come to find a guide," Emaye told the girl of seventeen dry seasons.

"A guide? To where?" Akosua persisted. Her curiosity was not satisfied.

"Ghana," Emaye answered.

"Ghana as in Africa? Oh my God! It's gonna be my first time," Akosua exclaimed happily. She was both nervous and excited. All her life, she had been conflicted beacause she would watch tv and saw how the western world portrayed Africa. It was always negative, with malnourished children playing in mud or people acting in savage-like ways. However, when she was a child, Pa Shango would tell stories to the children of the small towns. He told stories about the great things Africans had done, and all the children dreamed about going one day.

"It's beautiful, not at all like what you see on tv," Emaye said to Akosua as if she had read her thoughts. "It's the home of humanity," Emaye continued, and Akosua smiled at the thought of Africa.

"So, where in London are we going to find this guide of ours?"

Akosua asked Emaye, who was busy looking at the zooming cars. Emaye waited a couple of minutes to respond.

"Oh, sorry. It just amazes me how fast these automobiles are moving. We are going to Brixton," Emaye replied, "It's one of blackest neighborhoods in town."

"Do you know the person, or will it be a random stranger on the street?" Akosua asked jokingly.

"A random stranger on the street," Emaye responded in a dead serious tone.

That alarmed Akosua. She had only meant it as a joke. "What?! You know I was just joking right? A stranger is not a good idea. We won't know the person and what if he or she tries to harm us?" Akusua questioned with caution and worry.

"I'm just joking too. You can relax, Akosua," Emaye said with a huge grin on her amused face. Akosua sighed with relief. "We are going to take the underground. Come on, Follow me."

"The under what?" Akosua looked confused.

"It's the metro or the subway or whatever you call it," Emaye said laughing with mirth.

"We don't have that in Barbados," Akosua replied, joining in Emaye's laughter, "So, I don't know how to call it."

Some might have said it looked like a mad girl laughing by herself and giving into the pressure of loneliness. However, the simple truth was they were just two beings enjoying life's humor. It was raining when they arrived in Brixton. Akosua watched black women, men, and children run to find a dry place. It reminded her of Barbados and its rainy seasons when she and her sister would sprint to find shelter. They would laugh at the top of their lungs if the rain touched them. Akosua missed Ina dearly.

"So many black people here," Akosua remarked.

Emaye nodded as she looked at the street signs. "I told you," she replied with a smirk. Akosua was about to suggest that they should shelter themselves from the rain when Emaye snapped her fingers, and a tall black umbrella appeared in her hand.

"Whoa," Akosua gasped at the unexpected act, "I thought you were going to cut down on your powers," Akosua said with worry and winced, remembering what happened in China.

Emaye smiled, the umbrella perched over her head. "My powers are stronger here. More believe the ocean has spirit, I feel strong," This seemed to comfort Akosua.

"Well, be careful," Akosua cautioned as Emaye grinned. They both continued their journey through the rainy city. They walked for about fifteen minutes until they passed a stunning white library and came face to face with African archives.

"It's here," Emaye muttered to herself, just loud enough for Akosua to hear. "Let's go in." They walked to the glass door of the archives and opened it. Emaye motioned for Akosua to go inside. The room was vibrant. There were beautiful African paintings and masks of lions and landscapes covering the walls. A couple of people sat at tables in the indoor café, laughing and listening to music, mainly afro beats. It was lively a place, "Come on," Emaye called as she walked toward a staircase. "Follow me."

"Excuse me," snapped a woman sitting behind a desk that Akosua and Emaye had not previously noticed.

The woman had long brown straight hair that clung to her back and her nose was pointy and her skin was pink like a pigs. "What do you need help with young girl?" The woman glared directly at Akosua.

The woman was an unbeliever. She could not see Emaye. "What do I say?"Akosua whispered quietly to Emaye.

"Tell her you are looking for Kwabena."

"Can I help you?" the woman repeated with annoyance in her voice.

"I'm here for Kwabena," Akosua replied, annoyed with the woman's rudeness.

"Do you have a meeting scheduled?" the woman pried.

Akosua looked at Emaye for conformation and watched her shake her head yes. Akosua looked a little feeble, "I do have one," she told the impatient and rude woman. Akosua wondered why a person like the woman worked at the archives. The woman looked bored and uninterested.

"Go up then," the woman told Akosua.

Once up the set of stairs, Emaye broke down laughing, "It's clear that the lady pissed you off," she said to Akosua who shook her head with displeasure for the woman.

"How can I not be, when you are dealing with rude people? I was so tempted to slap her across the face for being so impolite," Akosua fumed at Emaye who just giggled.

"The library is over there." Emaye pointed to an enormous door at the end of the dim hallway and they made their way towards the door.

"You know, it must be fun being invisible sometimes. You don't have to deal with rude people," Akosua noted.

Emaye studied the teen with amusement. "Yea, but being invisible can make me weak," she replied.

"Yes, but no rude people," Akosua said with a kindhearted smile. Emaye smiled back.

Emaye knocked on the door that had the sign "Library" written on it. However, without waiting for a reponse, she pushed open the door and a young man stood by an enormous shelf filled with books. He was stunning. It was as if his skin had stolen the moon's glow. His deep brown eyes were soft. His lips were round like the sun. Akosua was mesmerized by his beauty. He reminded her of a piece of art that one could study all day. Akosua stood staring at the young man. Emaye noticed and nudged the dazed teen.

"Something caught your eye I see," Emaye said with a chuckle, Akosua lit up with embarrassment, which encouraged Emaye to laugh even harder. The young man glanced at the two.

"Hello, may I help you with something?" he asked politely, His voice was deep and melodic. It sent butterflies flying through Akosua's stomach.

"Yes, hello. I'm Emaye and I'm looking for Kwabena," Emaye told him.

He smiled brightly putting his white teeth on display. "Oh, Emaye!

Ayele has told me loads about you. I'm Kwabena." He walked over to Emaye and embraced her in a hug she could not refuse.

"This is Akosua," Emaye told a joyful Kwabena who in turn gave Akosua a merry smile which made the teen almost melt.

"It's lovely to meet you." he said as he embraced her in a warm hug. Akosua couldn't seem to form words, so instead, she smiled in response. He was a gem to her eyes. "So, you are the chosen one, huh?" Kwabena asked Akosua bluntly.

"Yea, I suppose," she replied quickly with a nervous awkward laugh.

Kwabena studied the girl of seventeen dry seasons for a few seconds and finally said simply, "Nice."

Akosua wondered how he knew, but she would ask Emaye about it later.

"Kwabena, Akosua and I are planning on going to Ghana in four days time. We really need a guide and a way to speak to the government, can you help us? We would pay all expenses," Emaye asked Kwabena with courtesy.

Kwabena laughed. "Governments in Africa can be so corrupt, they would never listen to what you have to say. Most of our presidents are the West's puppets," the young man said with honesty. This made Akosua uneasy. "In order to make a difference, you would have to talk to the native Ghanaians and you would have to convince them." Akosua's heart dropped, the journey seemed more and more impossible. "But I will take you and help you best I can," Kwabena said ending his monologue. Akosua slowly took a breath and felt herself fill up with hope again. Both Emaye and Akosua smiled with gratitude. "My lunch break is approaching. May I take you two out to eat?" Kwabena asked kindly.

"That would be really nice actually," Emaye replied while Akosua nodded in agreement, her stomach rumbling with hunger.

"Perfect, you both can wait for me downstairs. I will be down shortly." Emaye and Akosua thanked him again and made their way downstairs.

"Back already?" the unmannerly woman asked Akosua. "That sure was quick. What was the meeting about?"

Akosua had enough. She walked straight to the woman and said with a cunning smile on her face, "Yea, it was quick, and the meeting was about impolite and nosy people like you." The woman fell silent and became redder than the reddest tomato.

"Ok, I'm here. Ready?" Kwabena announced as he walked down the last stair.

"We are," Emaye replied. Akosua turned away from the rude woman and once again, was mesmerized by the sight of the young man.

"Follow me then," Kwabena said softly and walked to the archives' exit.

"Come back back to earth," Emaye whispered to Akosua as she waved her hand in front of the teen's face.

"Ahh, I don't know why I do that," Akosua said a bit annoyed with herself.

"I know why. You have a crush," Emaye told Akosua with a mischievous grin.

"No, no, no. That's not true. Stop that Emaye," Akosua exclaimed, burning with discomfort. Emaye shook her head, walked up next to Kwabena and started an amiable conversation with him. It was drizzling outside.

"I will take you to a Jamaican restaurant," Kwabena announced.

"Not a Ghanahain one?" Emaye asked jokingly.

"Hey now, I'm a Pan–African and plus, in Ghana we will have time to eat at plenty," Kwabena responded with a hearty laugh. Akosua had never heard the term Pan–African and felt awfully timid to ask what it meant. They walked through Brixton for a while, until they arrived in front a little red, black, and green restaurant called *Irie Vibrations*. "This is one of my favorite spots in London," Kwabena said after the three of them were seated in the back of the busy and popular restaurant. Haile Selassie posters decorated the colorful walls while Bob Marley's music played in the background.

"Thank you for bringing us here," Akosua spoke up finally, after being unusually quiet.

"It's my pleasure," Kwabena said with a charming smile. The restaurant seemed to be filled with believers. As a result, Emaye looked strong and stunning "So, when you were chosen, how did you feel? Did you feel prepared? How do you feel now?" Kwabena asked Akosua many questions.

She opened her mouth to speak but Emaye interjected candidly," She was not ready when I met her. She had a lot to learn and still needs to learn a lot." The words stung Akosua and hit her right in the guts. She thought of all she had to sacrifice for this journey. She could not understand why Emaye would say something so hurtful. Akosua tried to let her anger slide, like water down a banana leaf, but Emaye's words stuck with her and her guts ached. The food arrived and the three of them started to eat, but suddenly the patty and rice and beans seemed less appetizing to Akosua, She distanced herself from all conversation. he even grabbed her half-broken phone from her jean pocket and turned it on. It was the first time since she left Barbados that she had turned it on. Hundreds of messages from her family and friends flooded her phone. Her head buzzed and she sank further into her chair. She wanted to respond to all her messages to let everyone know that she was alive, that she was ok. Sadly, Akosua knew she could not.

"Akosua!" Emaye exclaimed and frowned at the girl of seventeen dry seasosns with disappointment. "What are you doing?!"

Akosua felt ashamed. She quickly turned off her vibrating phone and placed it back in her pocket. "Nothing, sorry," she replied quickly, knowing that she avoided a response.

Kwabena politely smiled at the ordeal. "Well, ladies my lunch break is almost over. I will start heading back," he said as he waved over the waiter to pay the bill.

"We can't thank you enough," Emaye told him with gratitude, "We will be in contact for Ghana."

He nodded, got up gracefully, and gave Emaye and Akosua a hug and went off swiftly. Once Kwabena was out of sight, Akosua let her words pour out, "So you think that I'm not ready?" she asked, visbly hurt.

Emaye's face became grim, but she said in a gentle tone, "I think you still have a lot to learn."

Akosua's heart sank again."After all I have sacrificed and all the pain I had to go through? Do you think leaving your home country or family and friends is easy? Having to go to sleep every night wondering if your family thinks you are dead is not fun," Akosua said with a sheet of icy pain that made her throat hurt.

"Look Akosua, I know it's far from easy for you and I'm not trying to hurt you, but do you still have doubts about this journey? Do you have doubts about being the chosen one?" Emaye asked, seeing how sorrowful and frustrated Akosua was.

"Of course, I do! I don't see an end to this journey or any progress. I'm just seventeen dry seasons, what do I know about the world?" Akosua exclaimed as tears threatened to pour out of her eyes.

"Can I get you anything else?" the waiter asked but Emaye just nodded her head no and the waiter stalked off.

"Listen, you can't have doubts. Doubts are the key to failing. You were chosen because it's your destiny and you have to learn to accept it. This journey is bigger than you and, Akosua, age is a state of mind, you have to remember that. This journey is not just about warning humans to stop polluting the oceans but also to make them aware of how sick of a society they live in for encouraging wastefulness and harming nature," Emaye explained truthfully and wisely to Akosua. Aksowa took a breath and the two of them sat in silence for a moment which seemed to relax her upset emotions. Akosua continued to breathe and the more she did, the more it sounded like the waves of the sea.

CHAPTER 5

IT HAD BEEN two whole days since Emaye and the girl of seventeen dry seasons had been outside. They stayed locked up in a little apartment they rented in a neighborhood that went by the name of Camden. Akosua felt trapped. She was not used to being enclosed for so long. In Barbados, the houses were always open and there was a sense of freedom that Akosua could not find in the apartment, no matter how deep she searched. "Can we go out, Emaye?" Akosua asked for the fith time that morning.

"We need to meditate and reflect," Emaye would respond each time.

"Agh, but I have not seen the sky in days. I want to fill the sun on my skin," Akosua complained.

"Akosua, let's be rational here. It's raining outside and the sky is dark grey. I promise that you won't find the sun," Emaye said. "We will go out tomorrow."

"Now I know what exile feels like, "Akosua muttered quietly, feeling nostalgic. Suddenly, a thought crossed her mind. "Emaye, if your mother is Yemanja, then who is your father? Are you human?"

Emaye smiled, as if she were amused by the question. She put down the book she was reading and said, "Akosua, I'm one hundred percent human."

Akosua wore a perplexed expression. "You are?" the girl of seventeen dry seasons asked, a little surprised.

Emaye sighed and said, "Yemanja is my spirit guide. She is my protector and the divinity that was responsible for bringing me on earth."

"Oh gosh, I had no idea that existed but what about your human parents?"Akosua asked, astounded.

"They died when I was 16," Emaye coughed and continued, "I had a sister who died before I was born. After the death of my sister, my parents asked Yemanja to gift them with another child. Yemanja gave them me with the condition that when I was sixteen, I would live with her for a year, learning from her, and cut off from humanity."

What Emaye told the girl of seventeen dry seasons was all so strange to hear and hard to fully comprehend. "I'm very sorry about your parents. It must not have been easy," she told Emaye with empathy, a basic human trait that many lacked.

"It wasn't. One day your beloved walked the earth and the next day they vanished from it. The sad thing is that you never lay eyes on them again You never touch them again. Yemanja kept me alive, Akosua. My faith in her kept me up and strong." Emaye winced while she talked about the scars of her past, the heavy burden her heart had to carry.

Akosua really felt Emaye's sorrow when she spoke. "I can only imagine,"Akosua said with sadness. "What is your spirit guide?"

Emaye laughed a little when she responded, "It's something you are born with. Many people have spirit guides but do nothing to activate their relationship with their divinity. They tend to not know they have one, or sometimes they are afraid of having one."

Akosua was given so much food for thought. "Do I have a spirit guide? Is Yemanja the only spirit guide?"Akosua asked intrigued.

"Oh no, not at all. There are so many, but Yemanja is one of the main ones. You have Ogun, Oshun or Freda, Shango, Oya, Dantor and many more."

Akosua was engrossed by the conversation. "But how can you tell which one a person has?" Akosua questioned.

"You can't always tell right away You would have to get a divination, but sometimes you can guess by someone's characteristics. For example, if someone's spirit guide is Ogun, they tend to get angry quickly. They live for justice and usually tend to be leaders and can be excellent blacksmiths," Emaye explained to Akosua.

"What about Ohsun, how do you tell?"Akosua asked extremely captivated.

"Oshun is the goddess of beauty, love, and fresh waters. When people have her as a spirit guide, they usually are beauty queens or kings. They are amazing flirters and love rivers. Some might say are a bit narcissistic," Emaye responded to Akosua who made mental notes.

"Emaye, do you know who my spirit guide is?"Akosua asked extremely impatient to hear the response.

"Take a guess,"Emaye laughed.

"Me? I have no clue," Akosua exclaimed.

Emaye smiled softly and simply said, "Who is the divinity that picked you for this mission?" The girl of seventeen dry seasons stayed silent, the truth biting at her. "Yemanja?"Akosua asked with incredulity.

Emaye nodded and asked, "Why so surprised?"

It was true, Akosua was very puzzled. "I just don't understand Emaye, I'm just so confused," she said with a long sigh.

"You can't question it, Akosua. It was decided before you were born," Emaye told the bewildered girl of seventeen dry seasons.

"But Yemanja has not showed any sign," Akosua whispered.

"Listen, Akosua, the fact that she chose you for this mission is a huge hint. This should be a time of reflection for you. You now know the truth." Emaye spoke with conviction and passion, and it was an inspiration to Akosua, "Once you start to really believe that she is your spirit guide, you will receive dreams and visions." Akosua was bemused. She never knew or imagined that spirit guides existed and never thought that she would have one herslf, and that it would be Yemanja of all spirit guides. "Now, let's meditate," Emaye said breaking through Akosua's chain of thoughts. The two of them sat on the red carpeted floor and closed their eyes. "Repeat after me," Emaye told Akosua:

"Yemanja give us the strength and courage
Justice to fight injustice
To accept the things that we can not change
Let us ride your waves to victory
Give us light when we cross a dense forest
Give us your wisdom to overcome the obstacles of the world
Blood for blood
Water for water
Harmony to overcome chaos
Mother ocean the bed of creation
The foundation of creativity
Your power flows through my veins
I owe my life to you
I am you

They spent the rest of the day chanting and taking slow and steady breaths. It was so relaxing for Akosua, and she loved it. Emaye amazed her by elevating candles in mid-air with the flick of her finger. It was a beautiful sight. "When Yemanja initiates you, you are given powers," Emaye told Akosua noticing the teen's awe and admiration.

"What a gift," Akosua whispered softly. Emaye got up and put some tea on the stove for the two of them. They sat peacefully, drank tea, and talked for hours. Akosua saw many sides of Emaye that increased her fondness for the young woman even more than before. They laughed and made jokes, and Emaya told Akosua about the many trips she had been on. She also shared sorrowful stories about being an orphan in Brazil. Akosua told Emaye about her family and friends. Talking about them was therapeutic for Akosua.

"Tomorow, I want to show you something in London," Emaye said with a loving smile. "It will remind you of Barbados."

Akosua happily smiled. "Really, what is it?" she asked excitedly.

"It's a surprise. You will see tomorrow," Emaye answered with a good-natured laugh. The next morning, the sun had come out of its hiding place in the clouds. It was the first time in days that Akosua saw blue sky. "Go get ready. I want to leave soon," Emaye told the sleepy girl of seventeen dry seasons, whose eyes were red from somber.

"Ok, I'm going to take a shower. I'll be really quick," Akosua replied in a drowsy voice. Akosua grabbed a towel and made her way to the bathroom. As she walked, she felt something cold and uncomfortable run down her spine. She quickly opened the bathroom door and screamed at the sight that awaited her.

On the bathroom's mirror, painted in what looked like blood were the words, "Stay out or death awaits!" Emaye heard Akosua's screams of terror and ran straight into the bathroom and gasped. Akosua had collapsed on the ground and was trembling. Emaye touched Akosua's forehead. "Oh Yemanja, this is not good," she muttered to herself.

"What's going on Emaye?"Akosua asked as her voice quivered.

"Shush, don't worry it will be ok," Emaye said softly but the teen wasn't quite so sure. "Go back to the living room. I have work to do in here." Akosua nodded and allowed Emaye to help her get up. Emaye stayed in the bathroom for an hour before she came out.

"Emaye, what was that?"Akosua asked quietly. She was sitting on the coach, her body rigid with fear.

"Some people are trying to stop your journey from happening," Emaye responded calmly and with seriousness.

"What?! But why?" Akosua asked agitatedly.

Emaye sat down on the couch next to the teen. "Akosua, please stay calm. This is all new to you." Emaye sighed. "In the world of the divinities, there are people who choose to do bad with the powers their spirit guide blessed them with. They put spells on people and just make life a living pain. They create havoc."

Akosua buzzed. She stayed as silent as night before breaking her silence and whispering in fear, "So black magic?"

"Don't use the term 'black magic,'" Emaye corrected, "Not everything that is dark or black is evil. Let's call it evil magic." Akosua was taken aback by her response. "The western governments hire people who do this evil magic to attack people like us," Emaye explained to Akosua.

Akosua was stunned. She tilted her head with incredulity. "Why would the western governments hire them?" she asked, utterly and completely bewildered.

"You have to understand that it's complicated. They do it to stop people like us from making others aware of issues going on. They want to keep the masses confused and unaware. People like us are a threat to their poisonous society, therefore we must be eliminated,"

Emaye explained in a serious tone, which made Akosua shake. "The people who work for those governments and do dirty deeds are called spiritual traitors," Emaye continued, "This journey will be harder than I thought, but we will get through it." Akosua shuddered at Emaye's words. "Akosua, listen to me. I want you to know that no matter what, you are protected, but sometimes you might receive dreams that will torment you or you might hear disturbing voices and feel strange things. Just keep going and don't let them get to you," Emaye said in an extremely serious tone. Akosua shook her head while her heart swelled with fear.

"I would have never thought the western governments believed in magic, Emaye. How did they find out about this mission?"Akosua asked, her fear pushed aside for the moment.

"They have spies everywhere and they are afraid of magic because they know of its power and what it can do. Since they're obsessed with dominating the world, they have to keep their guard up," Emaye told Akosua, who was busy trying to process all she had just heard.

"Emaye, how in the world are we going to convince mundanes to stop polluting the oceans if they are our enemies?" Akosua asked bitterly.

"We are not going to convince them. We are going to convince the people who are the victims of their society," Emaye replied confidently and her assurance, comforted the teen. Akosua walked over and gave her a warm embrace. Emaye smelled like a mixture of the sea and tropical flowers. She smelled like Barbados and the familiar scent slowy removed Akosua's fears. "Come on. I still have to show you. Go get dressed," Emaye reminded the teen. Akosua was quite happy, any excuse to get away from the apartment, and away from what had just happened.

The sun was still shining brightly when Akosua and Emaye took their first step outside. However, the commotion that morning dimmed Akosua's day. Once they arrived at the nearest train station, Emaye handed Akosua 20 pounds and told her, "Go get youself a ticket. Direction, Kew's Garden." She pointed Akosua toward the ticket machine.

"Why are we going to a garden?" Akosua muttered to herself. Twenty minutes later, Akosua and Emaye found themselves on a train heading to Kew's Garden. Akosua kept glancing around nervously to see if there was any threat. "So, you are taking me a garden, huh?" she finally asked, trying to get her mind off worry.

"Ever heard of a surprise?" Emaye said with a smirk. She had noticed the Akosua's anxious behavior, so she started asking her questions. "Akosua, tell me about Barbados, and what you like to do there."

Akosua smiled at the question. "I would surf a lot, actually. My friends and I would spend hours out on the ocean. It was relaxing and therapeutic. Or sometimes I would pick fruits with my siblings, or help my mother cook, and practice the guitar with my dad."

Emaye had a huge grin on her face. "Oh, I have always wanted to learn how to surf."

Akosua smiled. "Maybe I can teach you one day."

"That would be lovely. Please continue," Emaye replied with a sweet smile.

"In Barbados, the houses are open and tend to be very colorful. The sun is usually shining and the roosters are always singing. You will always hear music playing. In the evening, people go out and sway to the music or play dominos." Akosua smiled and laughed as she talked about her island.

"It seems wonderful," Emaye expressed.

"It really is, but have you not been there?" Akosua asked curiously.

"I only stayed for a short while, so I didn't see much," Emaye replied. She was about to add something, but they reached their destination. "Oh, we are here," she said and got up from where she was sitting. She headed to the train's exit and, as Akosua followed, her red coat nearly got stuck between two seats. They exited the train station, and walked up a block before coming face to face with an enormous black gate with a "Kew's Garden" sign. Many people were entering and the queue to purchase tickets was extremely long.

"We'll be standing here for ages," Akosua complained as she usually did. Suddenly she let her legs buckle.

"Now, let's not be fatalistic. Here, give me your hand," Emaye told Akosua. She took Akosua's extended hand and chanted a few words in a language that sounded both familiar and strange to Akosua's ears.

"Oh, oh. You are doing the thing you did when I first met you," Akosua said, a bit skeptical. Emaye ignored her. Slowly, Akosua felt her body lift into the air and swirl until, "Boom!" she felt her body hit the ground. Her head felt dizzy, so she kept her eyes shut until the lightheadedness passed.

"You can get up now. You are not hurt," Emaye said in an amused tone. Akosua spread her eyes wide open and stood up abruptly. She saw that she was on the other side of the gate and far away from the long queue. "Come on, follow me," Emaye told Akosua once she was done brushing the grass off her coat "That's a pretty coat by the way," Emaye added sweetly.

"It's my little sister's. It was too big for her, so she gave it to me," Akosua said. She smiled at the thought of her sister. She missed her so much. Akosua fought down her sadness. She observed the garden and beautiful flowers. Plants and trees grew strong. Crowds of people laid on the evergreen grass. "My sister would love this place," Akosua said softly.

"It's a beautiful garden," Emaye replied as she continued to stride forward with grace. Akosua was impatient to know where Emaye would take her. A few strides later, they came across a huge green-house. Emaye walked up to the entrance and pulled open the door. "I hope this will remind you of something you miss dearly," Emaye stated. Once Akosua stepped inside the greenhouse, a gust of humid air greeted her. Coconut trees grew tall alongside beautiful and ripe banana trees while papaya trees glowed. Akosua beamed with joy.

"Emaye, this reminds me of Barbado! It's so beautiful!" Akosua exclaimed with pure joy.

"This was my surprise, so I'm glad to see you like it." Emaye smiled warmly.

"I love it!"Akosua insisted as she walked over to smell the colorful tropical flowers that had caught her eye.

Akosua was pleasantly surprised to see so many tropical plants. "Who created this place?" she asked curiously as she continued to walk through the greenhouse Her amazement grew stronger the more she saw.

"A queen of Great Britain and Ireland," Emaye replied.

Akosua stopped and laughed, "An English queen did this? She grew tropical plants?"

"She was not just any queen. She was black and went by the name of Charlotte Sophie," Emaye explained.

Akosua almost choked on air. She was astounded. "A black queen you say?" Akosua asked in disbelief.

Emaye nodded. "Yes, she was the wife of King George the Third. She ruled between 1761 and 1801, I think."

"What?! How come people never hear about this queen?" Akosua questioned.

"Most truth is usually hidden," Emaye told Akosua as if it were normal and common knowlege. Akosua shook her head. "Do you know this queen was mocked for her African features? She would appear in newspapers with an enormous nose. They would draw her with outrageously large lips." As Emaye explained the history to Akosua, one might have said she was dropping gems. "It's the same racism blacks have faced for centuries and are still facing today."

The girl of seventeen dry seasons stared in bemusement and scratched her head. "The hatred is chilling," she whispered.

Emaye was silent as she walked over to a flourishing bush of lemon grass. "Some people say she had healing powers and that she used the plants in here to make medicines," Emaye said aloud.

"Do you believe it?" Akosua asked, burning with curiosity.

"Well, just by looking at these plants and herbs and being a healer myself, I know that they have healing properties, so that may very well be possible," Emaye replied as she studied a flower intently.

"How amazing," Akosua murmured, her thoughts flying all over the place.

"This queen is a mystery. She insisted and encouraged people in the UK to stop consuming sugar because she knew a lot about the situation in Haiti and how badly the enslaved Africans were treated on the sugar plantations," Emaye continued.

"How did she know?" Akosua asked and sat down on a bench to give Emaye her full attention.

"Apparently, she was close friends with a French queen. What was her name again?" Emaye spoke softly and paused. "Oh, yes I remember. The queen's name was Marie-Antoinette. She was having an affair with an African from Guadeloupe, named Chevalier de Saint–Georges, who was also known as Joseph Boulogne. He was one of the best composers in Europe and even influenced Mozart. Anyway, he had visted Haiti many times with his father who was a wealthy planter. He told Marie-Antoinette about the horrid things he had seen, and she then told Charlotte Sophie," Emaye explained to Akosua.

Her eyes widened, she suddenly realized how much she did not know. "I've been deprived of the truth for way too long," Akosua finally said with sadness and regret.

"That's why it's your mission to restore it," Emaye said with a slight smile.

The young woman and the girl of seventeen dry seasons continued to walk through England's black queen's greenhouse, engrossed in their thoughts. Akosua breathed in the clean air and allowed her imagination to fly free once again. She had been impressed with Emaye's knowledge, and was grateful for it. The rest of afternoon was a pleasant one. Akosua and Emaye sat a quaint café and had Earl Grey tea and mouth-watering biscuits. The morning's ordeal seemed like a distant memory, and so Akosua's nerves had calmed down a little.

"The people from China responded, Akosua," Emaye informed the teen in a soft voice as she brought up a delicate topic.

"Really, and what did they say?" Akosua demanded.

Emaye sighed and calmly said, "That they apologize deeply, but their government is not willing to make any changes regarding ocean pollution. They said that they have not seen any damage to the ecosystem."

Akosua's heart dropped. "So I failed," she said, feeling defeated. Her head dropped to the ground.

"No, you did not. It's not over. We just need to have a new plan," Emaye tried to reassure Akosua.

"I spoke with passion. I gave my all. I thought they believed me," Akosua said with tears in her eyes.

"Stop!" Emaye shouted, which made Akosua quickly wipe away her tears. "Don't blame yourself and don't be defeated by this," Emaye told her in a serious but encouraging tone. "China is like the warehouse of the world. They produce millions of tons of plastic a year and ship it to other countries."

Akosua sniffed and asked, "So, what are you saying?"

Emaye took Akosua's hand, "What I am trying to say is that if we convince people in other countries to stop consuming plastic, and stop polluting, it won't be good for China economically, and they will have to reduce the plastic they produce or stop."

Hope glimmered in Akosua's heart again. "Everything about this mission just seems more and more complicated," she admitted as she took a deep breath.

"I know, but what is life without a little struggle?" Emaye asked and Akosua smiled because Emaye sounded like her mother.

"It's a life that has not been lived," Akosua replied and Emaye nodded at her response.

"Don't worry, we'll get through this," she said as she took Akosua's hand in hers.

CHAPTER 6

"COME ON, AKOSUA, we will be late for our flight to Ghana!" Emaye cried from the apartment's living room.

"Coming, coming, but can't you use your powers to get us there?" Akosua replied as she struggled to put on mascara.

"No, I only use my powers when necessary but if you could spend less time in the bathroom, we could already be at the airport," Emaye told the teen as she walked into where Akosua was. It was true, Akosua had spent more time than usual in the bathroom that morning. "Are you trying to impress someone?" Emaye teased. "Tchipp!" Akosua exclaimed but still her face was hot with embarrassment. Emaye took the lipstick that Akosua was struggling to put on and put it on Akosua's lips for her. "You know, we will be on a plane so you really can't impress Kwabena," Emaye laughed.

"Agh, you are so annoying," Akosua said and she pushed Emaye playfully.

"You want me to mess up your lipstick?" Emaye threatened and giggled as she held the lipstick to the side of Akosua's face. Thirty minutes later, they were in a black taxi zooming through the busy London streets, heading to the airport.

"Your teleportation would have been quicker," Akosua said playfully. Emaye rolled her eyes and continued to read the book that she held. They arrived minutes before the ticket counter closed. Emaye worked her magic on the lady at the counter, just like she did in Barbados. Once they passed through security and arrived at their gate, they saw Kwabena. He stood by a pole, looking quite elegant in a brown and gold dashiki. Akosua couldn't help but admire his handsome face. The young man warmly embraced them.

"It's so nice to see you two again," Kwabena said, his voice warm and kind.

"It's a pleasure to be in your presence as well," Emaye replied kindly while Akosua just smiled sweetly.

The three of them sat in an empty row of seats and chatted away. Kwabena was charming and he spoke with such sincerity. Akosua replayed every word that slipped out of his mouth to the point she did not hear the question he asked her. Emaye nudged Akosua's shoulder and said, "Akosua, Kwabena asked you a question."

The teenager's heart pounded with embarrassment. "Oh, I'm sorry. I did not hear," Akosua apologized.

Kwabena gave a full-hearted laugh and said kindly, "It's alright. I was just asking how you found London."

"It's really grey with many, many clouds," Akosua told him.

"Sadly, that's true," Kwabena agreed.

"The English made London seem like a golden city in Barbados. It's nice but not a golden city. I guess it is just propaganda," Akosua continued.

Kwabena smiled. "I like the way you think," he said.

Akosua's heart did a couple of backflips. It beamed with pride. Emaye, who had not said a word in the conversation suddenly gave Akosua a mischievous smile. "In Ghana it's the same. The English have made the people there fantasize about London," Kwabena explained to Akosua, not noticing Emaye's smirk.

"Flight 287 is boarding," a voice announced on the airport's speakers.

"That's us. Here we come Ghana!" Kwabena said and stood up.

"Yes, here we come," Emaye finally spoke. On the plane, to Emaye's disappointment, she had to sit at the very back in the only open seat. Akosua and Kwabena's row had already been filled.

"Gosh, who is gonna hold my hand when the plane shakes?" Emaye whispered to Akosua.

"Sing a song, close your eyes, or think of me," Akosua said jokingly. "No, but seriously, you will be fine."

Emaye gave one last helpless glance at Akosua, waved to Kwabena, and vanished among the airplane seats.

"Akosua, I think the window seat is yours," Kwabena mentioned to Akosua.

"Yep, you're right," she told him as she politely asked the elderly woman already sitting on the row's aisle seat to let her pass. Kwabena sat in the seat right next to Akosua's. She felt nervous about being seated next to him and she hummed quietly to calm herself. During the flight, Kwabena happily chattered away. Akosua did not mind. It allowed her to lose herself in her thoughts. She would occasionally nod and ask questions to appear interested and involved. The flight was long and bumpy, and Akosua worried about Emaye and how scared she must have been.

"You will love Africa," Kwabena told Akosua confidently. The girl of seventeen dry seasons shut her small eyelids and smiled. It was a toothless one but heart-warming.

"I know I will." Four words was all she told him as she slowy felt herself drifting into slumber. The fear of snoring in public made her attempt to stop herself from slipping into the world of unconsciousness, but Mr. Sleep had done his job. Akosua awoke when the sun was setting, and the aircraft was on verge of landing in Accra, Ghana.

"We are almost here," Kwabena said with excitement. Akosua peeked out the window and felt a rush of zing run through her. She saw houses, trees, cars, but more importantly she saw Africa.

"Kwabena, how often do you come to Ghana?" Akosua asked suddenly.

"About three times a year. I wish I could come more often. My parents live here," he admitted.

"No place like home, huh," Akosua said. She knew how he felt.

"You got that right. My dream is to live here someday," he confessed.

Akosua sighed, then said sullenly, "The day I return to Barbados, if I return, I don't think I would ever want to leave again."

Kwabena patted her on the shoulder and told her in a compassionate tone, "Don't worry, you will return." Akosua nodded with hope lingering in the valley of her heart. Five minutes later, the plane landed. She smiled wildly and brightly. She was finally in Africa. Finally in the Motherland. Kwabena and Akosua exited the aeroplane and waited for Emaye to come out. She emerged from a crowd with an enormous grin on her face.

"I feel strong. There are many believers here," Emaye announced. Memories of Pa Shango telling his stories about Africa ran through Akosua. She and Kwabena smiled at the vigorous Emaye in front of them.

"Give thanks," Kwabena replied with joy, and Akosua's eyes sent happiness to Emaye.

"Let's go save the ocean and the living!" Emaye said with excitement. They all laughed blissfully. All of a sudden, Akosua felt the cold and unpleasant thing run down her spine again. She shook with fear. Voices filled her head, whispering insults. They started to get louder and louder. Akosua's vision became blurry, and she dropped to her knees on the floor. It was the spiritual traitors. She felt powerless.

"Akosua, Akosua, please tell me you are alright," she vaguely heard Emaye say. The voices continued to drown Akosua's thoughts. Emaye chanted a few words and the voices stopped, leaving an unpleasant and terrible silence. Akosua opened her eyes with relief.

"It's them." She croaked out the words, her voice sore. Tears gushed down her ebony cheeks. "I could do nothing. I did nothing Emaye. I'm scared," Akosua agonized.

"Breathe," Emaye said as she caressed Akosua's head and spoke her words as soothing as the ocean, "I know it's scary, but we will get through this." Kwabena kept asking in distress what he could do, but Emaye ignored him. She was too busy consoling Akosua. Emaye helped her stand up before they got too much unwanted attention focused on them. "Nothing, Kwabena, everything will be fine," Emaye finally told the young man. He sighed with relief when he saw that Akosua was on her feet again.

"Thanks," Akosua said gratefully to Kwabena, her voice frail and her eyes red. She was *bouleversee.* They passed through immigration without any problems beyond the huge and noisy lines. Emaye was visible to many. Accra was busy. Cars, and moto taxies zoomed by, leaving trails of dust. Many people walked with pots on their heads, baskets in their hands, and children on their backs while others just walked and chatted away. Akosua was familiar with the famous Afrob beats that played loudly on the streets. Ghana was a place of life. It felt human and earthly. Akosua kept her head pressed against the taxi's window as she looked out into the world. Her silence kept everyone tense. Emaye sat next to her and occasionally rubbed the her shoulder while Kwabena sat up front next to the friendly driver. They were on their way to a luxury hotel located at the center of Accra.

"So how does it feel to be in Africa?" Kwabena asked nervously, as he tried to break through the unpleasant silence.

"It's exhilarating," Emaye admitted. Kwabena nodded happily. Akosua stayed silent and, in truth, no one expected her to speak.

"It feels as if I've been here before," Akosua finally said.

"I mean, it is the Motherland," Emaye said with a sly smile. Akosua nodded. She was surprised when the taxi stopped in front of what looked like a palace. It was grand and stunning. A large sign was perched at the top. It read, "Kwame Nkrumah Hotel."

"We're here." Kwabena announced. Akosua and Emaye got out of the taxi.

The girl of seventeen dry seasons was mesmerized by the hotel's beauty. "When you said the hotel would be nice, I did not think this nice!" she told Emaye, dumbfolded.

Emaye smiled and said, "We are in Africa, sweetness, home of queens and kings." Akosua smiled at the words, feeling grateful to be in Africa. The driver and Kwabena got the suitcases out of the taxi. They thanked the driver, a kind older man, and Kwabena handed him a 10,000 Cedi bill. The driver's wrinkles formed into a beautiful grateful smile, he waved goodbye as he got back into his car. Kwabena, Akosua, and Emaye dragged their suitcases into the hotel's lobby. Inside, it was bright. A huge chandelier made of diamonds hung from an all white ceiling. Chairs covered with Kente cloth were spread out in the lobby alongside glass coffee tables.

"Hello, how can I help you?" one of the women working behind the desk asked.

Kwabena spoke to her in Twi. His words slipped quickly out his mouth. The woman smiled and replied to him. Twi sounded like music to Akosua's ears and she regretted that she could not understand a word of it. The woman handed Kwabena a key. She called out to a man standing at the hotel's entrance, and directed him to their luggage.

"Come on, follow me," Kwabena told Akosua and Emaye. They followed Kwabena and watched him and the man who was young, short, and in very good shape, carry the suitcases up many flights of stairs. It was ironic that such a luxurious hotel had no elevator. They arrived in front a massive brown door.

"Well, ladies this is where I leave you," Kwabena announced while he handed a key to Emaye.

"Oh, you're not staying with us?" Akosua asked with a tiny hint of disappointment.

"I'm afraid not. I'll be staying with some of my cousins," Kwabena told her.

"Well, Kwabena, thank you for everything," Emaye spoke.

"I have not done much yet, but it's my pleasure. The hotel will provide you with dinner and breakfast. Tomorrow, I will be here at nine and will bring you to the market to buy African clothes. You know, just to seem more convincing when you speak to people," Kwabena said with a smirk.

Akosua looked down at her jeans and her red jacket. She noticed how out of place she would be when speaking to women and men dressed in beautiful African clothes. "I think that's not a bad idea," she agreed, and Emaye laughed.

"Well, see you tomorrow," Kwabena said as he waved them goodbye and disappeared down the many stairs with the young man by his side, chatting away in Twi.

"Let's go in," Emaye said to Akosua. She pushed open the door and they entered a large room. To Akosua's surprise, it was simple. The walls were wide and painted white. Pretty orange curtains hung over a window. The room looked odd compared to the flamboyant lobby.

"It's simple,"Akosua remarked.

Emaye was amused by her words and said, "Well, sometimes the simplest things are the most complex."

Akosua smiled at Emaye's adage. That night, she watched a star dance with the moon through the window. It was the first time in a while that she watched the gems of the sky. Emaye was sleeping deeply, and strangely enough, her snores appeased Akosua. Just the presence of another human being comforted her. The night was short-lived. Emaye was the first to rise. She shook Akosua's shoulder gently to try to wake her from a deep somber. "Shake that tiredness out of you. Ghana is ready for you," Emaye said with a sweet little laugh.

Akosua opened her beautiful brown eyes and burst out laughing. Somehow, Africa made her heart light and peaceful. "You and your sayings," she sputtered as she attempted to control her warm and contagious laughter. It was too late. Emaye became a victim of this laughter, and they laughed until their guts hurt and they could laugh no more.

"Ah, Yemanja! Laughter is so healing. It's music to one's ear," Emaye finally said. "Now, let's go eat breakfast before Kwabena arrives." They got dressed; Emaye in a plain white tunic with pretty cowrie shells that adorned her hair, and Akosua in a royal blue shirt and blue cotton pants. They were elegant and went downstairs and ate an extravagant breakfast in the hotel's grand dining room. Many women and men were eating and chatting away in Twi while a couple of tourists looked a bit out of place. A waiter came by and served Emaye and Akosua eggs, bread, yams, plantains and more. Akosua thanked him and devoured her food. Emaye just giggled at Akosua, who made it seem as if she had not eaten in days.

As they finished, Kwabena appeared. He wore a beautiful yellow and green African shirt. He waved at them from afar before he walked over and sat down at their table. "Morning, queens. How did you sleep?" he asked with a smirk that made Akosua smile brightly and Emaye laugh. The handsome young man was such a charmer, and Akosua noticed how the women in the room gazed his way.

"The queens slept well actually. Thank you for asking," Emaye answered Kwabena with a smile.

"It was short though, but how did you sleep?" Akosua asked.

Kwabena sighed sarcastically. "I had an amazing night of sleep, but I mean, man, the chickens woke me up so early," he said. Akosua and Emaye nearly died of laughter. Akosua almost melted when Kwabena tapped her shoulder playfully. "I'm ready to help you save the world," he declared.

"Well, we are ready too," Emaye announced.

"Let's do it then," Akosua declared and for the first time, she felt ready.

Ghana was filled with life. It was so different from England's gloomy skies and with everyone being stuck in their own little box.

Akosua felt free as she rode on the back of a taxi moto. She could hear her heart singing with joy as the moto sped past people, cars, and trees. "I love this," she cried to Emaye who sat behind her with her locks dancing with the wind. Kwabena sat on a moto taxi behind them, smiling with all his teeth out. They reminded Akosua of the pearls she used to find on Barbados's shore. The taxi moto slowed down as it reached an area with many cars and motos. Vendors on the side of the road sat selling their wares. It was the market, and it was huge. There were many people selling, buying, talking, and haggling, of course. The market was congested with people, taxi motos, cars, people with pots on their heads, and men pushing carts of plastic soda bottles.

As they got off their taxi motos, Kwabena said in a serious tone, "Ok, ladies, this is an African market. So, if you see something, make sure you haggle for it 'cause if you don't, you will pay an arm and a leg for it." Emaye and Akosua nodded. In Barbados, Akosua had much experience in haggling. "Ok, let's go adorn my queens," Kwabena said. Women sold beautiful fabrics of all colors, shapes, and sizes. It was pleasing to the eye. They spent hours in the market. They bought jewelry, fabrics, clothes, and bags. It was a pleasant first day in Africa, and Akosua's thoughts were far away from the spiritual traitors. Emaye and Kwabena were busy negotiating with a woman vendor. Akosua had gotten tired, so she sat on an empty bucket nearby to rest.

"Akosua, is that you?" Akosua froze when she heard a voice so familiar, a voice she had longed to hear ever since she had left

Barbados. It was the voice of Beeny, her best friend. Akosua turned around and almost fell off the bucket when she saw her beloved friends Beeny and Lettaya. They were standing with an older man a couple of feet away.

"This can't be possible,"Akosua muttered with shock. She closed her eyes and then opened them again. Beeny and Lettaya sprinted to Akosua and enveloped her in the most loving hug. Akosua breathed in her friends' aroma. The girls released Akosua and Beeny brought her hand to Akosua's face and smacked her. "Ouch, that hurts,"Akosua cried.

"Don't ever leave us again," Beeny said between laughs and sobs. In fourteen years of friendship, Akosua had never once seen Beeny cry. She was surprised to see waterfalls roll out her friend's eyes.

"Oh, Akosua, thank goodness you're ok. You don't look hurt or starving," Lettaya said, her long curly hair messy and her eyes blood-shot red.

"How did you guys find me?"Akosua asked her friends, still in disbelief. Before Beeny or Lettaya could respond, Emaye and Kwabena appeared.

"Akosua, what is going on?" Emaye asked curiously as she studied Beeny and Lettaya intently.

"Um, Emaye these are my friends, Beeny and Lettaya," Akosua told Emaye, still confused herself about the situation.

Emaye's face dropped as she said, "You told your friends you were here?"

Akosua panicked, "Emaye, no, I didn't tell them anything, I swear,"Akosua insisted.

"Akosua, why are you responding to her? Get away from those kidnappers. We are leaving," Beeny commanded, her words filled wih fire and determination as she glared and pointed in Emaye and Kwabena's direction. Kwabena looked confused and uncomfortable.

"Beeny, they are my friends. They are not kidnappers." Akosua tried to sooth her friends' anguish.

"Akosua, they brought you here and forced you to cut off your family," Beeny exclaimed,

"Don't let them brain washyou."

Akosua shook and tears threatened to burst out her eyes like a dam with too much water.

"Come on Ak. Let's go home to Barbados." Lettaya stepped forward as she spoke, her voice calm but strong.

"My loves, I'm so sorry, but I can't. Not now at least. It's complicated,"Akosua said, overwhelmed by many emotions. She felt her heart break.

"Akosua, what are they holding over you?" Beeny demanded and, with her eyes, she shot daggers of distaste at Emaye and Kwabena, "We traveled miles, spent many painful and sleepless nights to find you."

Akosua was at a loss for words. She could feel her friends' hurt and that pained her more than anything.

"Akosua, if you stay, we stay, and that's the end of it," Lettaya said in the same calm and determined voice.

"No, you can't. It's not fair,"Akosua protested but she saw her friends' serious faces and knew that they would not back down. Akosua saw that Emaye was on the verge of snapping her fingers to perform magic on her friends. "Wait,"Akosua pleaded with Emaye as she held her wrist, "Don't do it, please. My friends have to stay."

Emaye dropped her arm to her side and frowned. She whispered so that only Akosua could hear. "I don't know, Akosua, it will be complicated."

"Emaye, please let them stay. They are like my sisters and they came all this way to find me,"Akosua begged.

Emaye sighed and said, "I have to ask Yemanja permission. Give me a second." She pulled Akosua aside and placed four cowrie shells in her hand. "Close your eyes and count to seven." Akosua did as she was told. She could feel her friends' perplexed gazes. Emaye chanted a few words and told Akosua to open her eyes and hand her the cowrie shells. Emaye studied the shells with intent and finally muttered to Akosua. "Yemanja says they can stay."

Akosua sighed with relief. "You two can stay," she announced to her friends.

They smiled a toothless one and gave Akosua another hug. "Ak, we deserve an explanation now," Beeny insisted. "What in the world is all this?"

"And I promise you will get one," Akosua assured her friends, "However, I want to introduce you to my friends and not my kidnappers." Beeny and Lettaya nodded, "Beeny and Lettaya, this is Emaye and Kwabena and Emaye and Kwabena this is Beeny and Lettaya."

Beeny eyed Emaye and Kwabena curiously. "Hello, nice to meet you properly," she said politely, despite her prior outrage. Emaye and Kwabena in turn shook her hand and gently greeted her.

Lettaya, on the other hand, embraced both Emaye and Kwabena in a warm hug. "I'm sorry about earlier. Akosua looks strong and healthy and not like a victim of kidnapping," she told them. Lettaya had an instant connection with both of them. They smiled at her gratefully and Akosua's heart smiled at her friend because she had a natural gift for soothing things and building bridges between people.

After that day, the journey became more challenging but more beautiful. Akosua was happy to have her friends by her side. That night after the market, when they all returned to the hotel, Akosua told her friends the truth. She explained everything that happened to her. She told them about Yemanja and to her relief, her friends believed in the goddess. Akosua poured her heart out. She apologized for leaving Barbados without a word. Lettaya and Beeny were silent until Akosua was done speaking.

"I would've believed every word you just said," Lettaya told Akosua, and Beeny nodded in agreement. The girl of seventeen dry seasons sighed in relief and content. "Ak, why didn't you tell us?" Lettaya asked.

Akosua stayed silent and then said very quietly, "I was afraid you wouln't believe me, so I made the choice not to tell my family and friends."

Lettaya frowned, "Of course, we would have." She reassured Akosua.

Beeny's face lit up. "I knew it! I knew you were hiding something that night you disappeared at the beach," she said loudly, "But, man, going to a goddess's palace deep under the ocean?! How lucky you are!" Akosua laughed. The night at the beach felt like a lifetime ago but it happened only one month prior. One month since her world was turned upside down. "We missed you. Lettaya and I cried everyday," Beeny said with hurt in her voice. Akosua winced at the thought of her friends' pain. She wanted to ask about her family but that subject would be like a thousand needles stuck in her heart.

"So much is on your shoulders, Akosua. How do you cope?" Lettaya asked gently.

"Honestly, it's only quite recently that I've accepted this to be my destiny, but I would say faith is what kept me going, and still is. I had to understand that there is something higher than me, I had to believe Yemanja,"Akosua said, a bit afraid that she did not believe it. They all stayed silent, the sound of the traffic outside mingled with their thoughts."Now, can you two please explain to me how did you find me?"Akosua pried.

Lettaya sighed and Beeny yawned. "Oh, well the day you were supposedly kidnapped, Mr. Kame, Somalia's father, was walking his cattle and saw you run past him, so he followed you to the beach and saw you talking to this woman with locks. He turned around to care for one of his cows and when he turned back around, you and the woman had disappeared. No one in town knew who she was, so they thought you were kidnapped or dead. Beeny and I did not want to believe you were dead, so we started to investigate but found nothing." Lettaya paused. "We were desperate, Akosua. Day after day, we were restless, but one day we got the brilliant idea to track you by using the tracker on your phone."

"We saw that you were in London, England and we knew what we had to do," Beeny continued to explain the story. "You know, my cousin Mina who works at the airport? Well, Lettaya and I begged her to give us tickets to London."

Akosua was bewildered. "Do your parents know?" she asked. The last thing she wanted was more heartbroken parents.

"They think we are on a school trip to vist universities. They gave us money, but we are running low 'cause, we had to buy tickets to Ghana when we saw you were here," Beeny said. The girl of seventeen dry seasons was more than touched. Her friends had traveled thousands of miles just to find her.

"Wow, you girls really did all that for me?"Akosua asked, more than grateful.

"You are our sister Ak. We would swim across all five oceans if we had to for you," Lettaya told an overwhelmed Akosua. Emaye, who had gone downstairs to ask for an extra bed for Beeny and Lettaya, returned. She had been a little reserved after meeting Akosua's friends at the market, but Akosua knew that with time, she would warm up.

"Hey, are you girls hungry?" Emaye asked, "I was going to order dinner and then later we can go down and eat."

Akosua nodded yes and Beeny said, "Yes, super. We have money." Beeny reached into her pocket and politely handed Emaye a couple of bills.

"Don't worry, from now on all expenses are on me," Emaye said as she denied Beeny's money.

"Oh, wow, that's so kind but we can't accept," Beeny and Lettaya told Emaye.

"No, really, I insist," Emaye replied. They were pleasantly suprised and both thanked her. Emaye just nodded and walked out of the room.

Once she had left and had descended the stairs, Beeny remarked, "Wow, Emaye is so nice."

"I know, right, but we can't have her pay for everything. It's too much," Lettaya expressed.

"Don't worry, girls, Yemanja gave Emaye money for this mission to take care of our needs. We have more than enough if she even mentions to pay for all of us," Akosua told her friends. They did not look reassured, but Akosua said, as she took her friends' hands, "I'm just so happy you girls are here." She placed their hands over her heart to allow their love and energy to pulse through her soul.

CHAPTER 7

THE RISING OF the sun felt celestial, filling Akosua's eyes with life. The purple, orange and pink clouds painted the sky. Birds sang the sweetest melodies of life as Akosua, Emaye, Kwabena, Beeny and Lettaya stood facing a village. A long, red, dirt road stretched, allowing its dust to blow a greeting to the newcomers. Akosua was nervous. She pulled at her beautiful red and gold African dress to distract herself. "Just breathe," Emaye told her. Akosua did and felt slightly less nervous. It was a critical day. She had to speak to the villagers and the king of the village about Yemanja's warning. Stunning red brick mud houses stood parallel to each other, creating a pathway.

"Come on, ladies. Let's go change some minds," Kwabena said, and they all followed the striking young man. Akosua looked at her two friends for comfort. Beeny looked drowsy, but her majestic crown of kinky hair covered the drowsiness of her eyes. She smiled at Akosua. It was a smile filled with support and love. Lettaya, on the other hand, looked awake and alert. Her thick curly hair was pulled back, which gave a better view of her high cheek bones and the wide grin she gave Akosua.

Once they were in the village, many people came and greeted them. They came with friendliness and kindness. They were not the African savages with spears Akosua had always seen as a child on tv. Children, women, men, and elders came to say hello. It was special and the warm welcome melted away the rest of Akosua's nervousness. "Africa must be the kindest continent," Beeny whispered to Akosua and she smiled at her friend's comment, nodding her head in agreement.

Akosua watched a glowing Emaye. Her long locks intrigued many young children and, as a result, she found herself with multiple children in her arms touching and pulling at her hair. Emaye was beaming with bliss and Akosua was delighted to see her in that state. Akosua looked over at Kwabena who was engrossed in a conversation with several of the villagers. His warm and orotund voice filled the atmosphere. The young man caught Akosua's gaze and called out, "Welcome to Ghana queen!"Akosua smiled at him so brightly one could have mistaken her smile for the sun. Beeny and Lettaya laughed and danced with the many women and children.

Akosua's heart pounded with bliss. It was like a huge family reuniting after a few years of separation, but only this time it wasn't a few years, it was four hundred. Kwabena finally told Akosua, Emaye, Beeny and Lettaya to follow him to the king's quarters. The kind villagers created a path through their crowd so the visitors could walk to meet the king. They arrived in front of a massive, red brick mud house with images of leopards, lions, and birds carved into the walls. It was magnificent, Akosua thought to herself. A middle-aged woman waited outside. She politely greeted everyone by blowing kisses on eveyone's head. She was extremely pleased to see Kwabena and directed them inside the house. "Who is she?" Akosua asked Kwabena quietly.

"One of the king's wives," he replied.

"Have you met this king before?"Akosua asked, but Kwabena stayed unusually silent.

He finally said, "The king is my father."

Akosua almost gulped. She was shocked. "The king that we are about to meet is your father? Kwabena, how come you did not say anything?" Akosua questioned, but Kwabena looked a little sheepish.

"It's a long story," he replied. She simply nodded because she did not want to bother him with sensitive questions. Inside the house was breathtaking. There were beautiful bronze masks covering the walls. The sight was simply jaw-dropping.

"It's beautiful," Lettaya said as she gasped in amazement. Everyone, except Kwabena, agreed as they let their eyes travel the walls with awe. Kwabena simply looked to the ground, unbothered. *He must have grown up in the place*, Akosua thought to herself.

'It is," said a deep powerful voice. No one knew who the voice belonged to except Kwabena. The young man made his way toward the voice. He walked down the long corridor and motioned for everyone to follow. Kwabena pulled open the grand curtain at the end of the corridor and revealed a circular room. In the round room, sat a man on a throne. He was no more than fifty and looked majestic in his magnificent Kente cloth. He was the king, the very king Akosua had to convince. She trembled in fear. It was a fear of failure that haunted her hope. She was just a girl of seventeen dry seasons from Barbados. Who was she to persuade a mighty king?

"I know what you are doing. Stop thinking negative stuff," Emaye whispered.

Akosua jumped with surprise. "No, I'm not," she lied to reassure Emaye.

"Kwabena my son," the king said and Emaye looked at Kwabena with surprise and suspicion. Kwabena dropped to his knees in front of his father and held his hand. The king whispered something to Kwabena and then studied Akosua, Emaye, Beeeny and Lettaya intently. He finally asked,"Whom have you brought with you?"

"Father, Akosua has come with a message for you," Kwabena said and pointed at the girl of seventeen dry seasons. "These are her friends, Emaye, Beeny and Lettaya." The king grunted and Akosua cleared her throat nervousnessly.

"Hello, your majesty, I'm Akosua and I've come all the way from Barbados with a message to keep humanity safe," Akosua said. The king nodded and listened to her speak. Akosua spoke about the oceans' pollution causing harm to the fish and other sea creatures. She explained what would happen to humans if people did not stop polluting the ocean with plastic, fishing at uncontrollable rates, and dropping all kinds of toxins in the ocean. The girl of seventeen dry seasons was intimidated by the king's serious eyes, yet found comfort when she recognized Kwabena in the king's face. Akosua spoke with passion and conviction, and again being a natural, her words touched everyone in the room. Emaye gave Akosua supportive looks while Beeny and Lettaya were completely mesmerized by every word that poured out her mouth. When she was finished, the king stayed silent.

He opened his mouth after a few moments. "This is a difficult mission you are on, but not an impossible one," he said. "If the ancestors sent you, it must work." Akosua sighed with relief at he king's words. She felt a huge weight fall from her shoulders and onto the ground. The king continued, "I will forbid plastic in my village and will cut down on some fishing. I will pass the word to other villages and their kings. I don't know if they will change their ways, but I hope so." Akosua nodded with gratitude and thanked the king many times. The king knew a lot. He was a well of wisdom and was very kind as well, which made Akosua wonder why Kwabena had been so quiet about his father.

The group gladly accepted the king's invitation to dinner because they were terribly hungry. They ate yams, fufu, plantains, and a plethora of many other delicious foods. Akosua had never eaten so well in her lifetime. "These plantains are ten times better than the ones my auntie makes," Beeny said between two mouthfuls of food. Akosua and Lettaya sweetly laughed at her. Kwabena, however, looked a bit tense and Emaye was very quiet. Akosua frowned, saddened by Emaye and Kwabena's strange moods, but she continued to have a beautiful moment with Beeny and Lettaya. She had learned many things from the king.

Finally, when the feast was over and their bellies were more than full, everyone got up and thanked the king. "Thank you, King," Akosua said again with gratitude, "For everything."

He nodded his head kindly but said in a serious tone, "Stay strong, my daughter. I sense evil coming your way." Akosua trembled at the royal's words. She was overwhelmed with fear and looked at Emaye, who remained expressionless and silent. Beeny and Lettaya looked frightened, and Kwabena looke a bit ghastly. Everyone stayed soundless. After they said their last goodbyes to the king, they walked through the village where they received hundreds of *au revoirs* from the lovely villagers.

"I'm in danger," Akosua screamed in frustration once they were in the taxi van Kwabena had rented. They were heading back to the city.

"Calm down," Emaye begged Akosua.

"I can't, you heard the king!" Akosua screamed, "Evil is coming may way!" Her heart felt like it would explode. Beeny and Lettaya were alarmed but confused about what do.

"My dad tends to exaggerate, so it is probably not true," Kwabena told Akosua in an attempt to comfort her.

"It's not an exaggeration. When the awful voices fill my head, I can't control myself," Akosua cried as huge tears gushed down her face.

"Where there is life, there is hope. We will all be here to protect you. Always," Lettaya said as she reached from her seat and held onto Akosua's hand. Those words rang through Akosua's soul and reminded her of Barbados and her childhood. They reminded her of the oath that she, Beeny, and Lettaya had taken as children. She looked up and smiled at Lettaya. That's when it happened. The vehicle exploded. It burst into fire and all Akosua felt was her head exploding in pain. She felt herself drowning into unconsciousness. She felt totally powerless.

When Akosua opened her eyes, she felt a burning sensation on her arms and legs.

"Oh, thank Yemanja, you are awake," Emaye said with relief but in a feeble voice. She looked frail as she sat on a wooden stool. Akosua felt weak but looked around. She saw that they were in a little shack. Akosua also noticed that her arms and legs were slightly burnt.

"Emaye, what happened?"Akosua asked in a voice she barely recognized. She remembered when the van exploded, but that was all she recalled. Emaye shook as Akosua winced in pain from her burnt limbs.

"The van exploded," Emaye said so quietly one could hear a pin drop, "The spiritual traitors did it."

Distaste and anger flew wildly through Akosua's heart. "I hate them," Akosua said with rage, "Where are we and how long have I been out?" Emaye got up and pushed open the shack's door. The powerful ocean appeared in the near distance, and Akosua felt Yemanja pulsing through her veins.

"Benin. We are in Benin. We had to seek refuge at a friend's village by the sea. My friend, she is a healer," Emaye said as she studied the waves of the sea and looked intently at every little detail. Akosua sensed that Emaye was not telling her something.

"Emaye, tell me everything. I know you are not telling me something," Akosua said longing to find out, but Emaye stayed silent and continued to stare out at the ocean. "Emaye, tell me," At that time, the girl of seventeen dry seasons yelled out of desperation.

Emaye looked down, ashamed and hurt, as she struggled to find words. She finally uttered, "Akosua, Lettaya is dead. She's gone."

Akosua let Emaye's words sink through her soul. "No, you're lying," she told Emaye with a nervous giggle. Akosua rolled off the bed she was resting on and erupted into uncontrollable laughter. It wasn't sweet or joyful, it was laughter that belonged to someone who was in pure denial. Tears washed down her face as agony slowly started to fill her soul. "Not my friend, not my Lettaya," Akosua wailed in pain so horrendous, it was suffocating. Her vision became blurry, her mind faint and her heart heavy, swollen with sorrow. She pulled herself from the ground and pushed past a sorrowful Emaye, sprinting out toward the ocean. She could hear Emaye's faint voice calling her, but she allowed her feet to carry her on as if it would take her far from her pain. How could her sun, her beloved friend and sister, walk the earth one day and vanish the next? Akosua's pain sickened her to the core and she collapsed on the sand face first. She felt guilt, anger, and regret run through her. Lettaya would not have died if it were not for her, Akosua told herself. "Why did you let this happen, Yemanja?! You were supposed to protect me, remember?!" Akosua yelled out at the ocean. The waves just stretched their spines and tickled her feet, far from soothing her agony. She lay in the sand for hours. The sky was grey and gloomy, and the heavens started to pour as if crying with her.

"Ak," called an infirm voice. It was Beeny. She stood, her thick brown hair blowing with the wind. Her skin was soaked with the sky's tears. Her lips were pale and her pupils were colored with suffering.

"She's gone, Beeny. Lettaya is gone," Akosua sobbed. At that moment her own existence seemed insignificant. Beeny crouched down to Akosua and placed her hands in hers.

"I know," Beeny said, tortured.

"It's all my fault! All of it is!" Akosua screamed. She could not control the emotional storm that ravaged her heart.

"No, don't ever say that," Beeny replied sternly, but still anguish lingered in her voice. The rain continued to pour with such force one might've thought it would never cease. Beeny pulled Akosua to her knees and stared her in the eyes. "We have to be strong for Lettaya. That's what she would've wanted," Beeny said, her words raw.

"How can we go on after this?" Akosua asked. She was so lost and heart-broken.

"I don't know how, but we have to, because Lettaya did not die so you could fail your mission. She did not die in vain," Beeny said as she hugged her dear and beloved friend. "As long as we live, Lettaya lives." The rain stopped, the heavens stopped crying and the waves got less agitated. However, as the two friends sat back in the sand on the beach, they knew that their pain would remain for years to come.

The loss of a beloved friend and sister created wounds that cut deep into the flesh of their souls. Akosua's pain and shock prevented her from speaking for a week. It was raw pain, the kind that tended to hurt the most. Akosua would nod her head "yes" or "no" when she had to engage in human conversation. She slept many hours of the day and she barely ate because she did not have the force or the desire to. Emaye and Beeny cared for her. Emaye's healer friend who was a kind, plump, middle-aged woman, also aided. Akosua's silence became solitude and her sadness became her companion. Kwabena would appear from time to time. He looked shaken and his heart was bruised. He himself had burns all over his skin, but he would sit with Akosua in the sand for hours and listen to her complete silence. The week felt like an eternity and was pure torture for Akosua. Then one night, Lettaya came to Akosua in a dream. Lettaya wore a white dress that floated with the wind. Her hair was out and free and her smiling, kind face shone brightly. The friends stood face to face on their favorite childhood beach in Barbados. A single tear rolled down Akosua's cheek.

"Don't cry, love," Lettaya said softly.

"But it's all my fault," Akosua sniffled.

"It isn't, Akosua. It was my hour. Listen, Akosua, the more you cry the more I'm tied to Earth. I need to go to the spirit world to be at peace," Lettaya said.

"Life is so hard without you, Lettaya," Akosua expressed sullenly.

"Life without me?" Lettaya laughed. "Akosua, I will always be there with you and Beeny." They both stayed silent for a while.

"I don't have the courage or strength to continue," Akosua wailed.

Lettaya smiled and peacefully said, "That heart you carry is stronger than you think. Plus, Akosua, humanity is counting on you. I'm counting on you," she whispered powerfully and walked toward the ocean. "Yemanja told me to tell you to keep going, and remember, my love, you can find me in the waves and the sea, in the sky and the trees, but most importantly you can find me in you," Lettaya said as she plunged into Yemanja's oceanic arms.

"Don't leave, please!" Akosua pleaded, but it was too late. Lettaya had vanished into the waves. Akosua woke up that morning peaceful. Her voice had come back.

"You look rested this morning," Emaye said sweetly.

Instead of nodding Akosua said, "I do feel rested."

Emaye's saddened eyes filled up with relief and joy. "It's good to hear your voice."

"She spoke to me, she spoke to me," Akosua kept repeating.

"Who?" Emaye asked, her full attention on the girl of seventeen dry seasons.

"Lettaya. My beautiful Lettaya. She spoke to me and told me not to cry or she won't be free. She told me she would always be with Beeny and me, and that she lives through us," Akosua said. For the first time in a long time, a real smile formed on her lips. "Where is Beeny? I need to tell her," Akosua insisted.

"She's down at the beach," Emaye answered. Akosua sprinted down to the beach and found Beeny sitting on the thick sand, staring out at the horizon. "She spoke to me! Lettaya spoke to me Beeny!"

Akosua cried out in excitement. Beeny turned around and smiled. She was quiet but happy to see her friend speak again.

"She lives on," Beeny said, her eyes still sorrowful. "What did she say?"

Akosua's eyes were full of joy, "Beeny, she told me that she lives through us." It was a powerful moment, one that was bittersweet and one that tested human fortitude. Akosua replayed her friend's last words before she died. "Where there's life there's hope!" Akosua yelled at the top of her lungs to the heavens and the great sea.

"Where there is life there is hope!" Beeny joined in and the two friends yelled the phrase again and again until they both could no longer utter another word. One might have thought they were two lunatics, but in truth they were simply two human beings exorcising their pain.

"I'll race you into the water," Akosua challenged Beeny.

"Hey, that's not fair, 'cause you're already standing," Beeny protested, but Akosua did not stop. She had already dived into the ocean. She let Yemanja wash over her and allowed the goddess to take away her anger and agonies. Yemanja carried them far to give them her strength. Akosua emerged from the sea and swam close to the sand. Beeny had already left the water and was lying under the sun to dry. Akosua noticed a figure in the distance, approaching. As it got closer, she realized it was Emaye. Her hips swayed to the rhythm of life. Akosua rushed to meet her.

"You have Yemanja's glow. The blue looks nice on you," Emaye told Akosua gently as her thick locks played with the wind. Surely enough, to Akosua's surprise, she was glowing blue.

"Whoa, w-w-what d-d-does this m-m-mean?" Akosua struggled to form a sentence.

Beeny walked up to Akosua and Emaye. She immediately jumped back, "Oh my God, Akosua, you are glowing blue!" Beeny exclaimed both in awe and alarm.

Emaye laughed, "It's a blessing from Yemanja, it's a sort of protection." both Akosua and Beeny exhaled deeply and Akosua then tackeled Emaye in a hug. "Now, you are getting me all wet," Emaye said between giggles "Get off." Beeny laughed at Akosua and Emaye.

"Nope, plus water is your element,"Akosua teased. It was the sweetness of life; moments like that kept her going. They all walked back toward the many shacks spread across the beach. Some people were sitting, looking at the ocean or cutting fish. Akosua's pain was not gone, but it felt lighter. "It must be so nice to live here," she commented as she looked at the peaceful people enjoying life.

"Yea, I know, right; it must be stress free and peaceful," Emaye added and Akosua and Beeny nodded in accordance. They walked into the shack Akosua had been recovering in and sat down, drank lemon grass tea and talked.

"Where's Kwabena?" Akosua finally asked. The thought had been nagging her.

"He's staying in one of the men's shack, but he is not in the best state," Emaye told Akosua. "He is feeling weak from his burns."

So much had happened that Akosua didn't even have time to

focus on the others. "Oh, my goodness, were you two burnt? I never got the chance to ask. I'm so sorry," Akosua asked Emaye and Beeny worriedly. She felt guilty.

"It's ok, Akosua, you were going through so much," Emaye said, "I was burnt a little but not much, and, Emaye was untouched.". Akosua sighed with relief. She was so grateful that her friends had not been badly wounded.

Akosua turned toward Beeny and said, "I'm sorry, Beeny, that I wasn't there more. I completely ignored your pain."

Tears tumbled down Beeny's cheeks, "You were recovering from your wounds and grieving a friend. I was just grieving," Beeny said softly.

"You've always been so selfless," Akosua remarked quietly, "You've always been so strong." Beeny stayed silent, overwhelmed by the truthful compliments. "And you, Emaye. Thank you for being our mother and always carrying us," Akosua said with gratitude.

Emaye smiled tenderly in return. "I know that Lettaya meant the world to you girls, and I'm so sorry. We all know that she will walk with you girls forever," Emaye said sweetly, "'Cause sisterly love lasts for an eternity." Akosua and Beeny were both at a loss for words, and simply wrapped Emaye in a loving hug.

"I need to see Kwabena," Akosua announced.

Emaye nodded and asked Beeny, "Do you think you can take Akosua? I have to finish something."

"Yea, that's no problem," Beeny replied. Akosua and Beeny both got up. Akosua followed her friend out the shack. "Um, maybe we should've changed," Beeny said as she looked down at her wet clothes and suddenly Akosua's clothes seemed cold on her divine brown skin.

"Well, it's too late now, we are already out of the shack," Akosua said with a little laugh. The two teens continued their way to Kwabena. They arrived in front of a shack identical to Akosua's. Beeny entered without knocking and, of course, Akosua followed. Kwabena lay on a thin mattress on the floor and was sipping on a cup of what appeared to be tea.

"I brought someone," Beeny said when she saw that the young man had not noticed them. Kwabena turned his body around, a little startled, and he attempted to smile but instead winced in pain when he saw Akosua.

"Don't smile. It is clear that it is physically painful when you do," Akosua said jokingly. She walked to him and held his hand tenderly. "I am happy to see you too Kwabena." When had she gained so much confidence around the handsome young man?

"I'm glad to see that you're talking," Kwabena croaked. He looked weak and since he wore no shirt, his awful burns were visible.

"I'm so sorry, Kwabena. For all of this," Akosua said with guilt. Kwabena squeezed her hands back.

"It's not for you to apologize, Akosua," he said quietly. "The spiritual traitors are the source of this disaster."

"I want revenge," Akosua said with distaste and bitterness. They had committed a crime against humanity. They were the root of evil and had created a catastrophe.

"Which you will get," Kwabena reassured Akosua. The spiritual traitors had taken so much from her. They had wounded her beyond repair. Akosua promised herself that they would feel her wrath, one that was just and unforgivable. "I never thought I would hear you speak again," Kwabena said very quietly. "You were so hurt." It pained him to say the words but it was the simple and honest truth.

Akosua listened. She closed her eyes, and finally said,"Kwabena, thank you, for visting me when I was not well and for always staying with me even when I could not speak."

"I'd do it all again if I had to," Kwabena croaked and Akosua held his hands even tighter.

She finally got up, sighed and said softly, "Kwabena we will leave you to rest. Take care of yourself." Kwabena muttered that he would, and Akusua kindly squeezed his hands one last time before letting go.

"See you and stay strong," Beeny told the young man. He nodded with gratitude. Akosua and Beeny walked out of Kwabena's shack into the afternoon's blazing sun. It hit their skin, but a cool and gentle breeze chased the heat away. "I could stay here forever, you know," Beeny said to her friend.

"I know what you mean; it really feels like home but on a deeper level," Akosua agreed. "I can't even explain it with words." They both sighed. "Beeny, what are we going to tell Lettaya's parents?"Akosua finally asked the question she could avoid no longer. "How are we going to tell them?"

Beeny stayed silent and looked down at the sand as if she was analyzing every grain. "Her father won't even know the difference, but her mother and step-father will be devastated," Beeny said sadly. "But we have to tell them, Akosua. That's the least they deserve."

"I know," Akosua whispered resentfully. Lettaya's father was an English alcoholic who had abandoned Lettaya and her mother when Lettaya was five, and moved back to England where he had started another family. Every couple of years, he would send Lettaya a message suddenly remembering her existence. That was as far as their relationship went. However, Lettaya's mother, Afia, was the kindest woman. She only tried to do good, just like Lettaya's step-father, Chad. "Miss Afia is the sweetest woman," Akosua said sorely. "It will break her heart."

Beeny's head dropped. "I know but she deserves to know," Beeny insisted painfully. She rubbed Akosua's back gently. When they had come back to their humble abode, Emaye was engrossed in an intense conversation with Jahi, her healer friend. Jahi was the first to notice the two friends' arrival. She smiled at them with goodness written all over her face.

"It's nice to see that you are better, Akosua," Jahi said to the girl of seventeen dry seasons. Akosua nodded politely at Jahi's words. "Please, Beeny, Akosua, sit with us." Jahi invited them on the mat she and Emaye were sitting on. They sat down and Emaye moved over to create more space for the girls who were still a bit wet.

"We wanted to have a ceremony for Lettaya," Emaye told the teens. The adolescents stayed quiet with their thoughts.

"So, like a funeral?" Beeny finally asked. "Lettaya was disintegrated into ashes." Akosua winced. She could not imagine that the only thing left of her friend was ashes. It hurt.

"No, not a funeral but a rememberance ceremony. It is sort of like a rite of passage for her to get into the spirit world peacefully," Jahi explained. "The way it works in African culture is that when you die, your spirit goes on a journey for forty days until you reach the realm of spirits, and then you are judged."

The teens stayed silent, listening until Beeny finally said "I'm in if you are." She looked over at Akosua for approval.

"I'm in," Akosua said. This was the least she could do for her beloved and worthy friend who had sacrificed so much for her.

"Good. Tomorrow at sunrise then," Jahi told everyone as she got up and headed to the door of the shack.

"Jahi," Akosua called, and the woman stopped and looked at her. "Where in Benin are we?"

A yellow light glowed in Jahi's eyes, as she answered, "Ouidah. We are in Ouidah." The name strangely and powerfully resonated through Akosua's soul. She felt her body shake and powerful waves crashed through her. "It was one of the biggest enslaved African ports," Jahi added. Akosua was mesmerized. The girl of seventeen dry seasons saw images flash through her mind. She watched a young girl, about the age of four or five, happily playing in red dirt as she watched her mother gather fruits. Beeny waved her hand in front of Akosua's face, but her friend did not flinch.

"Um, Akosua, are you ok? What's wrong?"

Beeny asked, alarmed but Emaye touched Beeny's hand kindly and said, "Shush, it is ok."

Beeny did not look convinced. "She's having *déjà vu*," Jahi explained softly, and it was true. Akosua was deep in a trance. She continued to watch the young girl play and study her mother. The young girl had something more than love and admiration in her eyes. Akosua, the girl of seventeen dry seasons noticed the young girl's innocent eyes fill with confusion and horror as she watched her mother being beaten and chained by two white men. Akosua watched the young girl scream in horror, and felt as if it were her own screams. Akosua suddenly realized that she was the young girl. She was one of the many children who had to endure such atrocities. Her mother's wails of pain rang through her soul. It was the most heartbreaking sound she had ever heard. Akosua felt two evil and cold hands grab her by her tiny shoulders and pull her farther away from her beloved mother who continued receiving beatings from the cruel and inhumane strangers. She could barely hear her screams because they were muffled by her pain. She felt her little body being thrown onto something wooden and hard. She heard loud sounds of waves crashing against the wood. Her body was bruised and limp. Terrified, she looked around and saw almost all the people in her village chained and piled up on one another. She glimpsed into misery's eyes itself. It was her people so humiliated and tramatized. The sight was unbearable.

Akosua awoke from her trance. She felt Jahi, Emaye and Beeny's eyes on her. "I've been here before, but they took me and my people.

They took me away from my mother," Akosua sobbed. "I was a little girl and they took me and threw me on a slave ship." Akosua could feel her heart breaking. Emaye quickly wrapped her in a hug before she could fall apart. Akosua finally understood. She was an orphan who had been stolen, an orphan who had to endure hell on earth. She was an orphan who had felt chaos, who had to live for 400 years in unbalance and destruction. She now understood that her destiny was to restore balance.

"Maat, "Emaye said softly.

"Huh?" Akosua asked perplexed through her sobs.

"You have to restore it," Emaye said simply. "Maat is balance, harmony, and justice in Kemet." Beeny grabbed her friend's hands and kissed them.

"What's Kemet?"Akosua asked, her voice shaky and brittle.

"Black land. That was the original name of Egypt before it was invaded by evil peoples who sought nothing but destruction," Jahi explained to Akosua. "You are here to restore Maat. That's what you've come on earth to do."

Akosua let Jahi's words settle through her. No words could describe the emotions that were running through her soul. Perhaps there was no name, or perhaps those emotions were sent from the gods. Akosua understood that the mission Yemanja and the acestors had placed upon her shoulders would help restore some of the lost harmony. She finally saw what she had to see, and there was no going back. She closed her eyes and remembered what her mother used to say, "Life is a test." And it really was.

CHAPTER 8

THE UNIVERSE FELT different as the sun rose from the east. Life had a new meaning for Akosua. She held on to it as if it were a precious gem. No, she held on to it as if all of humanity depended on it. She felt at peace. Akosua sat around the fire with Jahi, Emaye, Beeny, and despite his wounds, a weak but present Kwabena. The flames of the fire danced wildly as Jahi shook her spiritual gord and chanted. They were not there to mourn Lettaya but to celebrate her life. Jahi's chants filled Akosua with powerful energy. She closed her eyes and Lettaya appeared dressed all in white. Lettaya danced with vigor, and as Emaye started to chant, Lettaya's dance accelerated. The fire blazed with passion. Jahi started to chant Lettaya's name and beckoned everyone to follow. Akosua felt the waves of the nearby ocean pulse through her, and the more everyone chanted, the more the energy grew stronger. It was such a relief to expel her burden and pain. A couple of the villagers gathered around the fire and watched with respect. A tall young woman emerged from the small crowd of spectators and placed platters filled with fruits and vegatables at Jahi's feet. "Akosua and Beeny," Jahi called, "These are offerings for Lettaya. Please bring the tray to the shore and let the water spirit take it away to her."

The two teens nodded and rose in silence and deference. Akosua took one of the platters from Jahi and walked toward the ocean. Beeny followed close behind her, carrying another platter. Akosua and Beeny placed the platters on the shore and watched the waves take the offerings. They watched until there was nothing left to watch. The friends returned to the fire where Jahi, Emaye, Kwabena and some villagers were chanting. They chanted for hours and poured a libation. Akosua no longer felt like a prisoner to her own pain. Once the ceremony was over, Emaye surrounded Akosua and Beeny in a loving hug.

"She lives on," Emaye whispered.

"She does," Akosua said, and she knew that this was the simple truth.

Jahi walked up to them followed by a limping Kwabena, "So what did you think?" Jahi asked softly, her voice seemed to dance.

"Lettaya would be happy," Beeny spoke first. "Thank you Jahi and Emaye, and you too Kwabena, for being here." Emaye smiled and Jahi nodded

Kwabena croaked, "I had to be here." They all stood silent.

"And you, Akosua. How do you feel?" Emaye asked.

Akosua sighed. It was a sigh of comfort. "I honestly feel relieved," she said," I feel as if I'm no longer a prisoner to raw and endless pain."

Jahi smiled tenderly, "That's what we wanted for you and Beeny," she said. "The ceremony wasn't just for Lettaya, it was also for the loved ones she left behind. It's to heal oneself." They stayed quiet and let the sea's wind blow on them. The villagers nodded their goodbyes and dispersed to their many houses on the beach and beyond.

That afternoon, the sun blazed as Emaye and Akosua sat outside their shack and sipped coconut water. Beeny was asleep and Kwabena was tending his wounds. Akosua let her eyes drown in the horizon. She felt peaceful and enjoyed the sun's warmth. "I know you could stay here forever," Emaye told the girl of seventeen dry seasons, "But you still have a mission."

Akosua sighed, "I really could Emaye," she responded, "I know, but the spiritual traitors have taken so much from me. What else will they take from me when I continue?" Emaye stayed silent, her thoughts flying, "I couldn't bear to put anyone else I love in danger again," Akosua added in a sad tone. "You've seen the disaster it created."

Emaye let moments pass before she spoke, "Akosua, how do you feel?"

Akosua was a little puzzled by the question, "I'm ok, I guess," she answered even though it wasn't entirely true.

"No, Akosua tell me how you really feel?" Emaye insisted.

Akosua hesitated, but then said, "Emaye, words can't describe how I feel. I honestly feel confused, sad, and shocked, but at the same

time I now know more than ever who I am and what my destiny is."
Akosua's words rang through her. Her truthfulness was liberating.

"That's all I wanted to hear," Emaye said softly. "Akosua, knowing
yourself and your life purpose is the first key of protection." Akosua
nodded and her eyes started to water.

"Emaye, I just don't want the people I care about to get hurt or
killed beacause of me,"Akosua insisted, her heart broken, "I just
wouldn't be able to bear it."

Emaye's eyes filled with pity then into a fire that Akosua had not
seen before, "I know, Akosua, but I promise on my life no one else
will get hurt," Emaye said fiercely. "What the spiritual traitors did to
Lettaya is unforgivable and I won't let it happen again."

Akosua was thankful and encouraged by the young Emaye's
words. "When do we leave this haven?"Akosua asked with a hint of
regret, "Where do we go next?"

Emaye got up. "Come," she told Akosua as she headed down to the
shore. A bit confused, Akosua followed the graceful woman. "Before
we leave, you have to do something," Emaye informed Akosua once
they had arrived at the shore and stood close to the enormous waves.

"What do I have to do?"Akosua asked, not sure what Emaye meant.

"Close your eyes." Akosua hesitated but did as she was told. Emaye
turned her around and forcefully pushed her into Benin's cool water.

"Emaye! No! What the heck are you doing?!" Akosua attempted
to scream, but she was muffled by the water that filled her lungs. She
felt something cold and scaly grab her by the leg. It felt familiar, but
it also felt like a lifetime ago. She felt herself blanking out and knew

where she was headed. She did not not resist the creature this time, knowing that it would be of no help. She became a calm victim. Akosua awoke and heard the same melodic voice that had changed her life.

"My child," Yemanja said, "It's good to see you."

Akosua's head felt faint but she could not help studying a floating Yemanja. The goddess was beyond beautiful, she was pulchritudinous. She smiled like the sun and her soft brown eyes could soothe the most agitated soul. Her beautiful locks were braided and a cowie shell crown replaced her golden one.

"Mother, do you like to kidnap people for fun?" Akosua asked.

Yemanja smiled, a bit amused. "Those are my ways," she plainly replied. "Relax my child." Being in Yemanja's presence was overwhelming. Her power was so grand, Akosua did relax. She felt Yemanja's energy traverse her soul, washing away all signs of stress.

"Mother, why have you brought me here?" Akosua asked Yemanja softly.

Yemanja smiled."You are doing well my child," the goddess told the the girl of seventeen dry seasons.

Akosua stayed quiet, submerged by a thought that had pained her. "Mother, you said you would protect me, but why did you let Lettaya die?"Akosua asked with the same hurt as a broken winged bird. "A part of me died when Lettaya died."

Yemanja's eyes glimmered at Akosua's words. "I am the water in your veins, Akosua. I walk with you day and night and protect you. My child, I am you as you are me," the goddess spoke with sincerity,

"But I can't interfere with destiny and dying was Lettaya's destiny." Akosua stayed silent. She replayed every word the goddess uttered. Akosua tried to accept and understand what Yemanja said, but for any human being it would be quite difficult. It was yet again another mystery of life that could not be solved. "My child, you have proven yourself worthy and have passed the biggest test, which is life. You are deserving, so I will give you special powers. They will assist you through the rest of your journey," Yemanja told Akosua calmly. "You have stayed strong where many have fallen."

Akosua shook. She was once again moved and couldn't seem to speak, "Me?" she finally asked, puzzled. "You are giving me powers?"

The goddess smiled. She was visibly amused by Akosua's incredulity. "Yes, little Akosua, you are a true daughter of Yemanja," the goddess replied, "Many are called, but few are chosen."

Life seemed to have taken a whole new form for Akosua. It was mysterious yet divine. "Use these powers wisely," Yemanja advised firmly. The goddess' omnipotent palms formed a small wave that she hurled at Akosua. Once the wave hit the girl of seenteen dry seasons, she felt an energy she had never felt before pulse through her veins like water in a river. No words could describe what she felt. It was just too powerful to explain. Akosua felt reborn. She felt complete. She felt herself become one with Yemanja. The most powerful waves of the ocean resounded through her soul. "You are my daughter," Yemanja said softly as her eyes twinkled brighter than any star of the night sky. A blue glow surrounded the girl of seventeen teen dry seasons. She had been reborn. "Now, take your powers my child, and free humanity from the chains of destruction," Yemanja instructed Akosua with a strong melodic voice.

With tears in her eyes, Akosua bowed in front of the goddess. "Mother, thank you. I can never thank you enough for what you've given me," she cried with respect and gratitude.

Yemanja looked down at Akosua. "There are indeed no words to describe this," the goddess said frankly and with much seriousness. After the thankful and tearful cries from Akosua, the goddess continued, "Now, Akosua, you will meet other children of the gods. They will be on missions like you. The other gods and I want you to come together and unite."

Akosua was startled. "There are others like me?" she asked the goddess in surprise.

"Yes, there are quite a few since there is so much chaos in the world my child. No one person can handle it," Yemanja informed Akosua.

"So, the other gods have sent their children on missions to restore balance, harmony and justice?" Akosua was shocked but she also felt less alone. She was amazed that there were others out in the world doing the same as she was. "I can't believe it," Akosua said.

Yemanja smiled. "Believe it my child and listen to me carefully," the goddess insisted, "There is a war going on, and when all the gods' children come together, they will become one powerful force." Akosua listened to her divinity. She knew the goddess was serious about everything she said. "Do you understand my child?" Yemanja asked an attentive Akosua.

"Yes, mother, I understand," Akosua responded with respect.

"Remember my child to unite. You must set aside your differences. I must also inform you that all the gods' children have different personalities which may create conflict," the goddess told the girl of seventeen dry seasons, "But you must remember to elevate yourself to a higher plane." Akosua let the words sink in. She felt strong and hopeful that she could overcome any obstacle on her path to victory. "It's time for you to return my child," Yemanja announced. Akosua frowned at the sudden news. She did not want to leave, but she knew it was the goddess' decision and she did not dare argue. "I've asked Emaye to teach you to use your powers," Yemanja informed her. She blew Akosua a kiss, "Goodbye for now my child."

Yemanja swirled water in her hand and chanted a few words.

"Goodbye mother," Akosua said softly as she felt her body being transported by the ocean. Akosua emerged with her heart filled with fervor. She was out quite far and noticed Emaye sitting on the shore peering out at the ocean. Akosua paddled her way to the sand, feeling vigorous and confident.

"You're back," Emaye called out with a smirk, "And you look strong."

Akosua smiled at Emaye who had tucked her long locks behind her ears. "I feel reborn," she replied. Akosua was glowing blue and was as radiant as the sun. She walked toward Emaye.

"That's because you are," Emaye told the girl of seventeen dry seasons. "You are a daughter of Yemanja and now my sister." Akosua was filled with gratitude as she looked into Emaye's eyes. She knew that Emaye could read her heart. It was a language that could not be heard and could only be felt.

It was a powerful afternoon. Emaye taught Akosua how to control and create the waves of the ocean. She also taught her how to heal and protect herself with the ocean's water. Akosua truly felt like herself, and a renewed sense of purpose ran through her. "Akosua, now that you have been given powers, you will become invisible or might feel weak when you encounter non-believers," Emaye warned the girl of seventeen dry seasons. The sun was setting, leaving a stunning trail of oranges on the dark blue sky. "Just remember to stay strong and remember who you are," Emaye told the thoughtful girl, "You might have to heal yourself but that I will teach you."

Akosua nodded and spoke, "Emaye, Yemanja told me that there are others like me. She said I would have to unite with them and that it would not be always easy."

Emaye stayed silent as she studied the horizon. "Yes, there are others like you and nothing will be easy," Emaye said without hesitation. "But you will manage." They started to walk back to their little but homely shack.

"Emaye, when will I meet them?" Akosua asked. Her thoughts were running wild and she was not able to tame them.

Emaye stopped, turned and looked at Akosua, before saying, "Ah, my friend, that's for the gods to decide."

Akosua wanted another response but deep down, she knew Emaye was right. The gods would in fact decide and she had to be ready for what would come.

CHAPTER 9

IT HAD BEEN two months since Akosua, Emaye, and Beeny had left behind the beautiful ocean village in Benin. Kwabena had retuned to England which had saddened Akosua tremendously. He had promised Akosua that they would meet again, but his words had not seemed sufficient to soothe Akosua. She really cared for the handsome young man and promised herself that she would confess her affection for him one day. If life allowed it. Akosua, Emaye and Beeny had traveled to twelve countries carrying out the mission. They went to Japan and talked about the 79,000 tons of plastic found in the Pacific Ocean. They also traveled to Nigeria and talked with the Ogoni people who were supportive and sympathized with Akosua. They visted beaches covered with seaweed caused by goblal warming in Martinique and Guadeloupe, and huge cities like Rio in Brazil which Emaye was especially fond of because it was her home. They went to ceremonies for Yemanja and the other divinities. They journeyed to Australia, Europe, and Canada to find how oblivious the people were on how much they participated in the ocean's catastrophe. Akosua felt productive and her powers grew stronger each day that went by. She was always filled with appreciation for Emaye and Beeny's presence and support.

They were in Ayiti, in the loud and very congested city of Port au Prince. The pollution stained the air but despite it all, people kept moving. Misery, people knew all about it. It was waking up without a gourd in your pocket to feed your family or not being able to pay for your sick and dying mother's medication. Despair also stained the air but the aroma of Ayiti being the first black nation kept the stains mellow. "Ayiti Cherie," Beeny sung a kompa song that she used to hear in Barbados as a child. Akosua's heart ached a bit. Being back in the Caribbean made her nostalgic of Barbados. They were all on the back of a motoclycle zooming through the crowed roads. They had backpacks that Emaye had found a way to make disappear then reappear. They were heading to Jacmel, a small town in the south of Ayiti that had beaches covered with plastic. "Motorcyles aren't really my thing," Beeny announced. She had been surprised when she found out Akosua had gotten powers, but with time, she got used to it. Akosua, on the other hand, loved motoclyes. She loved the fresh air that hit her skin.

"I love it," Akosua exclaimed, "It's exhilarating, Beeny." Akosua sensed that there were many believers in Ayiti and she felt her powers bursting. She felt free like an eagle in the sun-kissed sky.

"Ayiti is a special island," Emaye said. She had been in a pensive state and looked zen sitting at the back of the motoclyle with her eyes closed. Ayiti was truly beautiful, and one could feel that it was indeed a sacred place. Once out of the busy city of Port au Prince, they got to enjoy the pretty ranges of mountains and endless valleys. Many people stood or sat on the side of the road, selling cassava, bread, fruit and many other delicious and mouth-watering foods. Women carried baskets and large pots on their heads, which reminded Akosua of the things she had seen in Africa. The teen marveled at how the women kept such good balance. Akosua took in all the beauty. "How can such a beautiful place have such an awful past?" Emaye suddenly asked, her eyes still shut. Akosua and Benny did not know what she meant by that phrase.

"Emaye, what do you mean?" Beeny asked. She coud not contain her curiosity.

Emaye exhaled. "Well, first, with the Antillean genocide by Christopher Columbus and his evil men who decimated the entire indigenous population," Emaye said solemnly, "And, then, the enslavement and oppression of millions of Africans who were stolen from their land and forced to work in horrid conditions on sugar cane plantations. That's what I mean."

Akosua winced. She had never heard about the Antillean genocide, and the more truth she heard, the more the eyes of her soul opened. "I had no idea," Beeny said bitterly, "That's horrible, Emaye." The motorcyle sped up and the air got colder.

"It really is," Emaye agreed, "But we must be proud of the revolution that happened and remember the strength and courage it took." They stayed silent and reflected on Emaye's words. "Victory requires sacrifice," Emaye finally said, her words danced with the wind, covered in truth.

Jacmel was radiant and very peaceful compared to Port au Prince. Other motorcycles and colorful cars sped down the roads. The motocycle driver brought them to a hotel by a beach. The hotel was decorated with shells and pretty colorful stones. The workers at the hotel were friendly and welcoming. They brought Akosua, Emaye, and Beeny to an orange room with an ocean view. It was perfect for meditation for all of them. Emaye stared out at the huge body of water, at her mother, the great Yemanja. "You know, they said that many of the enslaved Africans, who came here were taken from Benin."

Akosua closed her eyes and thought of the little village that had helped her heal and changed her life. She remembered the déjà vu that happened to her and the profound ceremony for Lettaya. "I'm going down to the beach," she announced suddenly. The waves were begging her to come.

"Well, I'm going to take a nap," Beeny said. Akosua knew it was her friend's way of dealing with her painful longing for Lettaya.

Akosua nodded and looked toward Emaye, "What about you?" she asked.

Emaye took a while to respond. Her silence was deafening. "I feel something," she said all of a sudden.

Akosua and Beeny looked at her with surprise. "What is it? It's not bad, I hope," Akosua asked nervously. The room's red and orange curtains blew agitatedly. "It's not the spiritual traitors, I hope." Akosua felt a hint of fear and anger build inside of her.

"It isn't them," Emaye said, "I can't tell who it is, but they hold strong power."

Beeny looked fearful. The waves of the sea kept calling Akosua with each breath she took. "I'm going down to the water,"Akosua announced again, not caring about a possible threat.

"Akosua, I don't think it's a good idea," Beeny pleaded with her friend.

Emaye waved aside Beeny's pleads. "You can go but just be careful Ak," Emaye warned.

Once down at the beach, Akosua picked up shells and threw them far into the water. She felt one with the ocean. The sun was setting, leaving behind it a fiery orange and red sky. Akosua bent down to pick up another shell to throw when someone ran into her. She fell onto the sand and felt an electric shock run through her body. "Agh!"Akosua yelped. The person who had run into her had also fallen and had also cried with shock. It was a teenage girl with beautiful braids and a red cotton dress with a blue scarf tied to her waist. She kept her head down to the sand.

"No apology?"Akosua asked the girl, annoyed and not caring if the girl understood what she said. The girl snapped her head so fast, Akosua thought her neck would break. They stared at each other. The girl was no older than sixteen. The more Akosua stared at her, the more she felt a gush of energy run through her. The girl's head was oval shaped and her skin caramel. Her round eyes were home to fierce fires. It was as if Akosua had seen her before. "Who are you?" Akosua asked credously.

"A girl, can't you see?" the girl responded aggressively, and with no hint of friendliness.

"Tell me who you are," Akosua insisted, but the girl continued to stare at Akosua with defiance. The girl of seventeen dry seasons snapped her fingers and water appeared to be floating in her hands. She could hear the waves crashing through her soul so much that it was as if she was the ocean.

"It can't be possible," the girl whispered in total disbelief.

Akosua asked again, this time very calmy and peacefully, "Tell me who you really are."

The fires in the girl's eyes became stronger. She was radiant and her words were powerful. "I'm Amatamu, daughter of Ogun, the god of war and justice," she said with mastery and power, "I'm one of the children of the gods."

The wind blew wildly. Tthe ocean roared. The clouds clustered together and Akosua breathed. She inhaled the universe. She took it all in. She accepted the inevitable. Akosua felt the world lift her. She felt moved as she stared fixedly at Amatamu, a daughter of the gods. The girl of seventeen dry seasons realized then and there that she still had much to learn and understand. She had indeed many more dry seasons to live.

CPSIA information can be obtained
at www.ICGtesting.com
Printed in the USA
LVHW020703010719
622841LV00022B/1116